THE WAR-WAGON

THE WAR-WAGON

Lauran Paine

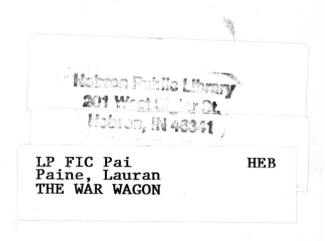

Chivers Press • G.K. Hall & Co.
Bath, England   Thorndike, Maine USA

This Large Print edition is published by Chivers Press, England, and by G.K. Hall & Co., USA.

Published in 2001 in the U.K. by arrangement with the author c/o Golden West Literary Agency.

Published in 2001 in the U.S. by arrangement with Golden West Literary Agency.

U.K. Hardcover ISBN 0-7540-4403-3 (Chivers Large Print)
U.K. Softcover ISBN 0-7540-4404-1 (Camden Large Print)
U.S. Softcover ISBN 0-7838-9324-8 (Nightingale Series Edition)

The text of this Large Print edition is unabridged.
Other aspects of the book may vary from the original edition.

Set in 16 pt. New Times Roman.

Printed in Great Britain on acid-free paper.

British Library Cataloguing in Publication Data available

Library of Congress Cataloging-in-Publication Data

Paine, Lauran.
  The war wagon / Lauran Paine.
    p. cm.
  ISBN 0-7838-9324-8 (lg. print : sc : alk. paper)
  1. Large type books. I. Title.
PS3566.A34 W37 2001
813'.54—dc21   00–047179

C H1   18·12·01

CHAPTER ONE

SOMETHING TO THINK ABOUT

When Old Man Dutra came into the Tenino Basin with four riders and three hundred head of unpredictable razorback cattle he had contracted for in west Texas and had not paid for, and had never had any intention of paying for, he was in his early forties; short, powerful, fearless, with black eyes, greying black hair and an arsenal of weapons in his oak wagon.

His first name was Manuel, but he was called Mike by his riders, and the people, few in number, who came to know him down in the town of Butterfield learned to respect Mike Dutra very early. He was irascible, would fight a buzz saw, had opened up the Tenino countryside to other stockmen, and went into his grave at the age of sixty-five, still unmarried, still contentious. But, having had slightly more than twenty years to do it in, had died a moderately wealthy man with four thousand head, at least fourteen thousand acres of deeded land—and he still had not paid for those first three hundred head of Texas cattle.

His heir, a nephew by the name of Richard Chase, came down from Nebraska where his mother had told him what she remembered of her brother—which was not a lot because she had married and left home while Manuel was still young—satisfied Butterfield's only lawyer and the township Marshal about his and his mother's identities, and had then ridden out to the Dutra ranch.

No one in Butterfield had seen Dick Chase for almost four months after that. His riders rode to town occasionally, on Saturday night, or at other times with a supply wagon, but Richard Chase did not ride in until the fourth month was about spent, and by then it was late in the riding season, with autumn in the offing, and with a noticeable bite to the early mornings and late evenings.

He was taller than his uncle had been, had tan instead of black eyes, and seemed quite unlike Manuel in physical appearance. No one in Butterfield knew how different—if at all— he was from Manuel in temperament. But he seemed different; he was a man who smiled easily and seemed to have a relaxed manner. When he entered Marshal Corbett's office tugging off a pair of worn-shiny roping gloves, he introduced himself, pumped Dan Corbett's big hand, took a chair, shoved back his hat and wrinkled his nose at the aroma of hot coffee coming from Dan's little blue-speckled pot atop the wood-stove. Then he said, 'It's been a hard damned summer, Mister Corbett,' and because Dan, who was a shrewd judge of men, decided he liked Richard Chase, he murmured

2

sympathetically; he had been a rangeman in his time. He knew what a hard summer was like.

He got to his feet, offering a cup of coffee, and while he was busy over by the stove Dick Chase studied the little cluttered room; its scuffed furnishings, the steel-reinforced oak cell-room door, and when he leaned to accept his steaming cup he said, 'I meant to get to town before this.'

He tried the coffee; it was too hot so he held the cup away. 'I never knew my uncle. His cattle were scattered from hell to breakfast. I guess he was a good stockman. I guess he had to be to put together a ranch like this one, but you know, Marshal, in Nebraska we been using chutes and round corrals for working cattle since I first hired out, and he didn't have anything out there that'd make it easier and quicker to run them through.'

Dick tried the coffee again. It was still very hot but he tasted it and nodded his head. 'You make a good brew, Marshal, and that's something a man very seldom gets when he's out with a wagon and his riding crew.'

Dan Corbett accepted the compliment with a slight smile. He had a feeling that Dick Chase had not ridden nine miles simply to sit in the jailhouse office sipping hot coffee, good or not. But big Dan Corbett, with his pale eyes and bulldog jaw, had learned, during his forty years of living, that a cowman could not be

3

rushed. Anyway, the office was warm, he had nothing in particular to do, and with plenty of time to make his assessment of the younger man, he was doing it as he looked at Chase and listened to him.

Manuel's nephew had a slightly hooked nose, shrewd and knowledgeable tawny eyes, a rangy, rawhide build, and Dan guessed him to be about thirty-five, and capable.

'When a man's new in a country,' Chase went on between sips of hot Java, 'he'd ought to go slow, feel his way, listen a lot, and keep out of other people's business.' He smiled at Dan. 'I sure had plenty of opportunity to do those things this working season.'

Corbett, feeling he should say something, agreed with Chase. 'A man don't often get into trouble actin' like that, Mister Chase.'

Dan Corbett had about decided Dick Chase was the kind of an individual who was a credit to any community.

'But,' said Dick Chase, gazing at the black contents of his thick white cup, 'in any cattle country I ever been in, there are rules.' The light tan eyes swept upwards to Corbett's face and the smile was gone. 'Mostly, I guess, when a new man arrives in a country, it's a little the way it was when we was kids goin' to a new school—someone has to test a man. Breakin' the rules is one way.'

Dan went after his second cup of Java and held out the pot, but Dick Chase wagged his

4

head and waited until the lawman was back in his comfortable old chair before continuing to speak.

'Some men can drink coffee all day long, Marshal, but I sure am not one of them ... Well, to get back to what I got to say: Do you know a man named Brackett?'

Dan knew Barney Brackett very well. Barney ranched south and west of the Dutra range. He was a laconic, turkey-necked, long-legged Texan who never seemed to be without a cud of tobacco in his cheek. Corbett had known Barney Brackett for about eight years; had shared drinks with him at Sullivan's saloon here in town, and had bedded down overnight at his home-place a number of times on his way back toward Butterfield when he'd been unable to reach town before midnight.

Corbett nodded his head. 'Know him well,' he replied.

Dick Chase shoved his legs out and gravely studied the scuffed toes of his boots. 'We made a tally as we worked the cattle,' he said quietly. 'Made two tallies in fact.' He continued to gaze at his boot-toes for a moment before also saying, 'I'm shy about two hundred head.' The tawny eyes swept up again. This was a characteristic of Dick Chase Dan Corbett would learn to know.

Marshal Corbett said nothing. The implication vas obvious, and it troubled him. He drank coffee and waited.

'I guess you know a lot more about cattle stealing than I'll ever know, Marshal, but in Nebraska I was raised with livestock, and we had our share of rustlers just like they have every other place where they got cattle.'

Dan thought, finished his coffee, and decided it was time to speak, so he put the cup aside and leaned on his desk. 'Mister Chase, Barney Brackett's got a lot of cattle. He hires about three, four riders each ridin' season just like your uncle used to do. He's been in the Tenino country as long as I have, and if you're leadin' up to maybe saying Barney stole your cattle . . .'

Chase met Dan Corbett's steady gaze with an equally steady one, and his smile returned, but faintly this time. 'No, Mister Corbett, I wouldn't make an accusation like that unless I had a lot of proof, and all I've got is my loss and—'

'It could be anyone, Mister Chase. Rustlers work through any big, empty range. We've lost a lot of cattle in this country.'

'Let me finish, Marshal. I've got my loss, and a peculiar situation. I'll tell you something you probably know as well as I do. There are two kinds of cattle thieves, Marshal. The kind that rides into a country and stays out of sight until they get to know the lie of the land, and which cattle they figure to rustle, then they swoop down, usually at night, and start their drive. They go fast and keep going. Sometimes

6

a crew can overtake them and sometimes it can't be done. That's one kind, Marshal. The other kind lives in the country where he steals cattle. He don't swoop down and run for it. He stays right where he's at. And he don't steal cows nor bulls nor big steers, he sifts through someone else's cattle cutting out big weaned calves, and he drives them maybe ten, twenty miles off to good feed, and leaves them there. He don't brand them. He only rustles big unbranded calves, the kind a riding crew goes lookin' for each spring and late autumn. He don't go near them often, and he don't put a mark on them.

'Marshal, big calves like that have been weaned. When you find calves how do you ordinarily prove they belong to you?'

Corbett answered shortly. 'By driving a cow wearin' your brand up, and lettin' her lick them and by lettin' them suck her—but if they're weaned she's got no milk and they don't suck.'

Chase's faint smile widened. 'Exactly. Big unmarked weaned calves belong to anyone who dabs a rope on them and puts his mark on them. That's an old rule of the range, isn't it?'

Marshal Corbett was motionless as he leaned, looking steadily at the younger man. He knew what was coming.

Dick Chase was still smiling when he said, 'Every big cowman loses a few head like that every season. He picks up a few mavericks that

7

way too. I guess it ordinarily about evens itself out . . . Two hundred big weaned calves is a hell of a lot of lost beef, Marshal.'

Dan Corbett could agree with that, but he didn't, he instead asked a question. 'Let's get back to Barney Brackett; where does he come into this?'

'After we made the tallies, and after a couple of my riders pointed out particular cows they had seen with little calves back earlier in the spring, but which had no calves now, we sort of wondered a little.'

'And?'

'We started riding, Mister Corbett. We covered one hell of a lot of country. Been at it for about three weeks now . . . Day before yesterday we found a mountain meadow about twenty miles southwest, back toward the big mountains that flank the range . . .'

'With cattle in it?'

'Yes. Almost two hundred head of big weaned calves without a mark on them, fat and sassy and perfectly content up there with feed to their bellies. That's why I rode down to see you; I don't know the boundaries very well. I'm not sure whose land that is.'

Dan Corbett let his breath out slowly and leaned back in his chair gazing at Dick Chase. 'If it's south and west, in foothills, or, for that matter, back about twenty miles into the mountains, it's Brackett's range.'

Chase kept smiling. 'That's about what I

8

figured, Marshal.'

'But, Mister Chase, I'll tell you something. Barney don't have to steal cattle. He's got a big outfit, plenty of riders, pays his bills, has a good reputation in the Tenino country; I'd make a guess that Barney's a fairly wealthy man. Whatever is goin' on, I'll lay you odds of a hundred to one Barney Brackett don't have a hand in it.'

Chase handled Marshal Corbett's nettlesomeness easily. 'I told you, Marshal, I wouldn't make an accusation unless I had proof. I've *got* proof—my big calves are in a hidden meadow that belongs to Brackett—but I'm not accusin' Brackett, not yet anyway. When I see some of those cattle wearing a raw, fresh Brackett brand, I'll have all the damned proof I need.'

Dick Chase arose and stood, thumbs hooked in his shellbelt, affably, and shrewdly, regarding Marshal Corbett. 'One reason I didn't ride in to see you the day after we got back to the ranch, Marshal, was because I figured you might be friendly with the stockmen around here, including Mister Brackett. I wanted you to know the whole story, but not with enough time to ride out there and maybe warn someone.

Dan Corbett leaned to arise, his temper coming up a notch.

They stood regarding each other steadily, with no smiles and no affability now.

'The other reason I rode in to talk to you today,' stated the cowman, 'was because now you know the whole story . . . except for this much more. You're not goin' to be able to suggest that you'n I ride out and talk to Brackett, and then go find my cattle and drive them back to my range, and that'll be the end of it because no one has put their brand on those cattle . . . Marshal, one of my riders watched Brackett's home-place from the hills. Yesterday they struck out with a wagon, heading toward the mountains . . . They're goin' up there to brand those cattle. *That's* the proof I need!'

Dick Chase went to the door, nodded, and passed out into the sun-bright roadway leaving Dan Corbett gazing after him. Very slowly, it occurred to Dan that Manuel Dutra's nephew was not only a knowledgeable range stockman, he was also damned clever. Maybe he was too clever.

CHAPTER TWO

HEADING OUT

Dick Chase was a working cowman; he employed no rangeboss, he filled that job himself, and when he got back to the ranchyard a rider in scuffed, worn old muleskin chaps was leaning in front of the barn watching Dick approach while he blandly smoked. His name was Sam Picket, and if Dick Chase had needed a rangeboss Sam would have been his choice. Sam was older than Chase, he was perhaps in his mid-forties, but he was one of those spare, calm, level-eyed men who could have just as easily have been in his mid-fifties.

When Dick rode up and swung off Sam said, 'We got the wagon ready . . . Did you ever look that thing over?'

Dick's brows went up a little. 'The wagon? No; it's just an old wagon, isn't it?'

Sam straightened up off the tie-rack. 'I want to show you something,' he said drily, and led off in the direction of the pole wagon-shed, which had three sides and a wide, full-length open front. There were two men down there, waiting. When Dick and Sam Picket walked up, one of those rangemen grinned widely. 'We got four horses ready,' he told Dick Chase. 'Two couldn't move this thing out of the yard.'

It was the truth—almost, anyway; two horses could have pulled the old wagon out of the yard, but they could not have pulled it up a hill nor held it back going down a hill.

Sam Picket dropped to one knee, lowered his head and pointed. 'Look under there, Dick. You never in your life seen a wagon with runnin' gear like that. Oversized stretcher, axles nearly twice as big as they got to be for

11

the size of the wagon, and oak sides over two inches thick.' He watched Chase lean down and look; then Sam got back upright, grabbed one of the sideboards and put his considerable strength into shaking it. It did not move an inch; it did not move at all, in fact, but if it had been any other wagon it certainly would have shivered under Picket's powerful heaving.

Sam put a frowning look upon Dick Chase. 'Did your uncle ever mention this wagon?'

Dick shook his head. He had never spoken to his uncle that he could remember, and if his mother had known anything about this very unique and obviously especially made wagon she surely would have mentioned it at some time over the years.

A cowboy who was leaning on the opposite forewheel looked levelly at Dick and said, 'I'll tell you what it is. When I was a button down in the Panhandle, I recollect seein' one of these things bein' drove southeasterly into Comanche country, by some Messican traders who told my paw they'd bought it off'n the widow of the feller who'd had it made. Them oldtimers used 'em. They had need for 'em. You could haul anything you wanted to in 'em; they was stout enough for anythin' you had a mind to load 'em with. But that's not what they was built for. Where I come from they called 'em "war wagons". Wasn't no In'ian arrer or no bullet could pierce the sides. Sometimes, my pappy told me, when folks got enough of

12

the damned raidin' they'd load a party of men into one of these things an' drive right down into In'ian country, and when they was attacked the fellers down inside would raise up and commence shooting—and nothin' could get through to wound nor kill 'em. War-wagons, folks called 'em, but this is the first one I've seen in fifteen—maybe twenty years.'

Dick knew that his uncle had come into the Tenino country many years earlier; he had to assume there had been hostiles in the basin at that time. It was also a safe assumption that before his uncle had reached the Tenino countryside with his razorbacks and his wild riding crew, he had encountered other hostiles, not necessarily Indians each time. If he could have known Manuel Dutra, even slightly, he would have understood better why his uncle would have gone to the expense of having a war-wagon built. If he had thought much about it at this time it would certainly have occurred to him that since his uncle had come this far, and had gone no farther, the Tenino country had been his destination, and nothing, renegades, Indians, floods, range fires, nothing under the sun was going to prevent him from reaching the basin.

He stepped back to look at another pair of rigs in the longshed, but Sam Picket began wagging his head. 'One's got all the steel tyres ready to fall off, an' we couldn't soak the wood soon enough to use the outfit. And that other old wagon—it's got a worn-through bed . . . It's this one, or go on horseback, Dick.'

The idea of taking the wagon had occurred to Chase shortly after sunrise when he had been saddling up for the ride to Butterfield. It would be twenty miles out and twenty miles back. Going out they could cover that much ground in a day, but returning with a drive of about two hundred animals it would probably take another day. He had decided to have a wagon hauled out, loaded and ready so that when he returned from town they could strike out.

One thing was very certain; if they did not get up there very soon those slick calves were all going to be branded, and what he needed was to ride up onto Brackett and his men while they were running on Brackett's brand. It did not happen often, with cattle thieves, but when it *did* happen, it was all the proof anyone needed to hang the thieves on the spot, or hand them over to the law. Dick wanted it to happen exactly that way. He was new to the country. People were waiting; they would pass no general judgment until he *did* something.

He wanted Marshal Corbett to arrive up there too. Otherwise he would not have gone to town to give Corbett the facts, but he did not want the law up there until he arrived there first. Now, he looked at the massively constructed war-wagon and was divided in his opinion about whether to exult or to laugh. Or to be disgusted because with an outfit like that he could not expect to make good enough time to reach the mountains before Corbett did, unless he did not stop for the customary rest-halts.

'Put the strongest horses on it that we've got,' he said to Sam Picket, and turned to the watching pair of rangeriders. The one who had identified the wagon was Frank Longtree. He was older than Dick but not any older than Sam Picket. He was a good hand. The other leaning man was a taffy-haired, blue-eyed younger man who had ridden in out of a spring storm and hired on under the name of Jim Jones.

Dick said, 'Where's Gus?'

Jones jerked a careless thumb. 'Gettin' up sacks of grub from the cook-house.'

Dick said, 'Saddle up, fetch along your carbines and coats and bedrolls. Toss your stuff in the wagon. When Gus comes along tell him he's to drive. Sam and I'll strike out now. You fellers come along with the wagon as soon as you can. Understood?'

Frank Longtree lightly scratched his chin. 'We got to leave this thing down below the mountains, Dick.'

Chase was reaching for his reins when he answered. 'Good. We'll use it for our base camp. Be sure you fetch along Gus's outfit an' an extra horse for him.' Dick stepped up and got settled. 'We'll keep watch for you. Let's go,

15

Sam.'

They went out of the yard at a steady walk. Behind them, a burly, squatty man emerged from the cook-house, scowled and bawled. 'Frank! Jim! Sure hate to wake you up, but I need some help with these grub sacks.'

When Longtree got over to the porch where the gorilla-built rangeman was standing, he glanced over his shoulder, watched Sam and Dick start loping northwesterly, and spoke as he faced forward. 'I figure he'd bring back the law an' a town posse.'

Neither the thick, unsmiling man nor Jim Jones answered. They shouldered heavy sacks and went trudging toward the war-wagon. When they put the sacks down Gus's thick, coarse features curled into a disbelieving look. '*That* thing?' he asked. 'We're goin' to take *that* thing?'

Frank stooped to pick up a sack and load it inside the wagon. 'It was that or go a-horseback, and Dick said we'd stay with the wagon . . . Jim, come lend me a hand gettin' the horses ready.'

Gus stood gazing at the functional, ugly, massive old wagon. In many ways he had been constructed along similar lines, but he must not have suspected it because he glowered at the wagon as he said, 'Of all the misbegotten vehicles I ever seen, you are the ugliest, the clumsiest, the sorriest lookin' and that's just for openers. I'll think of more to say after

16

we're rolling.'

They got the team on the pole, Gus climbed up, looked back once to be certain the tailgate was up and chained, looked forward at two big powerful rumps, kicked off the binders, flicked the flat side of the lines and said 'Well hell,' and whistled. The horses leaned into their collars.

Jim and Frank rode slightly ahead. Now and then one of them would look back. Eventually Jim said, 'Whoever built that thing sure had a grim heart in him.'

Frank Longtree looked surprised. 'Why would you figure that?'

'Look at that damnned thing, Frank. It's about as graceful as a big cub bear, but it's solid as rock and rolls in and out of the swales without a bobble. What would you guess that wagon weighs?'

'Hell, I don't know. A lot more'n any other wagon you ever saw, I expect . . . You never saw one before, did you?'

'No, I don't believe I ever even heard of one before, Frank.'

'That makes me feel old.'

Jim laughed. 'You *are* old, Frank.'

Longtree's even, reflective features creased into a rueful, slow smile. 'Yeah, I expect I am. But I'll tell you something, Jim—before we see that ranchyard again, you're goin' to be a lot older too. Not in the carcass, maybe, but sure as hell in the mind.'

17

Jones did not push for any explanation. He looked up ahead where Dick and Sam Picket were riding. Beyond them the land ran on for a considerable distance before it turned dark and rough where rocky foothills shaded back into rougher and timbered dark slopes and hazy peaks.

The distance was not formidable. It was respectable but not intimidating. To a man on foot it might have been discouraging, but that was why God had given a man two puny legs and a fair-sized brain, while he had given a horse four strong big legs and a smaller brain—so the man could cover greater distances off the back of a horse.

Sam Picket was bowed from horsebacking, and he was sagacious from having matured in a raw country where there was no mildness and little forgiving. He continued to gaze toward the mountains and worry his cud of molasses-cured chewing tobacco, calm, relaxed, reflective and constantly ready. That was what maturing on the frontier had brought Sam down to. There was one word to summarise it: capable. Sam Picket was a completely capable man. He had been facing crises of one kind or another all his life. He had survived them all, and had developed the knack for being able to look out for himself as well as others, and from this had come a variety of confidence only capable men had. He jutted his jaw and said, 'If Brackett's up there I'll eat my hat.'

'You saw his crew head up that way.'

'Yeah, but not him, and he's no fool. No man who has put together what Barney Brackett has, is fool enough to be at a hidden marking ground putting his brand on someone else's cattle. He'll leave that to his riders.'

Dick Chase also rode along watching the mountains. 'They'd have someone as look-out, I expect,' he speculated, thinking aloud, 'but unless he's got the eyes of an owl it's not going to help him much. We won't be close to those mountains until dark.'

For a while they were quiet, then Dick looped his reins and went to work rolling a smoke as he said, 'The only reason I can think of for a man as well set up as Brackett to steal a couple hundred of someone's cattle is because he's at heart a larcenous bastard. He's just got to steal something.' Dick lit up and trickled smoke. 'A thief is always one, isn't he? If we catch him up there runnin' his mark on our animals, we got the right to shoot or hang him. Sam, it wouldn't balance out if he was stealin' five hundred head. He'd lose five times what he might gain. How do you explain a man like that?'

'You just said it, Dick. If a man's got a black heart he's just naturally bad, and it comes out. What I was thinkin' earlier, while you was in town—a damned lousy thief don't steal once in twenty or so years. Why didn't he steal from your uncle?'

'Maybe he did and my uncle never knew it?'

Sam turned to regard his employer. 'From what I've heard in town about your uncle, he'd have known it if Brackett had been stealing from him, and he'd have killed Brackett for it.'

'Maybe he was afraid of my uncle. I'm new in the country, Sam. Like I told the marshal in town; people try other people, particularly they test newcomers.'

Picket jettisoned his cud. This conversation was going no place. He swung a hand to the cantle, twisted and looked back. Then he laughed. 'That is the damnedest lookin' outfit I ever saw. Look at that wagon, Dick.'

Chase turned, and also smiled. 'Looks like a big fir log with wheels stuck on it. I'll bet the In'ians rode round and round one of those things, feelin' frustrated as hell. They could kill the team-horses, but if the fellers inside had food and water an' plenty of ammunition . . . I wonder just how they *did* get the best of one of those things, Sam?'

Picket did not know. He straightened forward in the saddle and squinted at the location of the sun, then estimated about how many miles they yet had to cover before coming into the shielding foothills. Evidently his calculations were either encouraging or satisfactory because Sam smiled to himself a little, dug out his plug and worried off a corner of it.

The sun was red and low and beginning to give off a lot less warmth. It veiled the highest mountain rims with an almost unearthly glow the colour of diluted blood. Below where it touched, there was a deepening darkness which would be cold. An hour later when visibility had been cut back to about a half-mile, Dick raised a coated arm and pointed to a small, fitful spike of brilliance part way up the mountainside beyond the nearing foothills.

Sam said nothing. He chewed, and eyed the very distant campfire, and did not take his eyes off it for a long while. Not until he and Dick were past the first up-ended series of breaks and low rises which formed the rough foothills, and halted to wait for the war-wagon to reach them. They dismounted and buttoned their coats because it was cold in the foothills and before much longer it would be still colder.

CHAPTER THREE

TRAILS

Dick did not know the mountains. In fact he did not know much about Tenino basin outside of his own range; he'd only been in the country about four months and every day of that time had been spent working cattle or up-dating and reorganising his late uncle's ranch.

21

But Sam knew the mountains. Even when full darkness arrived and they went back to locate the wagon by its sound and lead it on up where they thought a decent camp could be made, Sam pointed out dim landmarks to Dick Chase; and when the wagon was in place with the big horses off the pole, the riders hauling their bedrolls out and buttoning their coats, Sam recalled anecdotes of this country up here, and some of the men who had worked for Manuel Dutra he had been up in here with.

Only when they were all hunkered down, bundled and eating a cold supper, and someone mentioned Brackett, did Sam become less than positive. He knew Brackett, he told them, had first met him about six or seven years back, but since that time although he had met a number of Brackett's rangemen from time to time, he had not really had a full conversation with Barney Brackett. In fact, he told them he had not seen Brackett in about a year.

In many areas this would have seemed unusual since the two ranches adjoined, but in the Tenino country where a next-door neighbour might be anywhere from ten to fifty miles distant, it was not unusual at all.

What had sparked the question had been someone's bafflement over a big, wealthy cowman stealing two hundred head of cattle. All Sam could say in reply was about what he and Dick had discussed on the ride out here. If

22

a man had larceny in his heart, he probably always had it, and had to exercise it now and then.

Frank Longtree dissented from that notion. 'Lots of men have stolen things, then changed and never stole again, Sam.'

No one cited examples of this, but they were all more or less satisfied that it was true. Then Jim Jones mentioned something different. 'We was on Brackett's range the last few miles, wasn't we, Sam?'

Picket nodded and raised a coat cuff to wipe his mouth.

'Where are his cattle?' Jim asked.

Again, no one spoke for a moment. Picket finally said, 'Maybe he's got 'em southward.' But Sam had not sounded convincing so Dick glanced at him. 'Does he usually take 'em south this time of year?' Sam considered his answer to this also, and finally yielded to indecision when he replied. 'Darned if I know. I *do* know that in years past when I've been in our upper country I've seen Brackett critters up here.'

Gus Hanson, who had been quietly eating, now brushed crumbs from his beard and began searching for his tobacco sack as he spoke. 'Depends on the year, don't it, Sam? If there's no rain a man wouldn't keep cattle in foothill country where there's no decent feed, if he had decent feed somewhere else.'

That was the truth. Dick also lit up. He

23

leaned back against a wagon-wheel gazing at Sam. 'This was a decent season,' he said quietly.

Sam threw up his hands and looked a little testily at Jim Jones who had opened this discussion. 'I got no idea where Brackett's darned cattle are.'

Frank Longtree hid a look of amusement by lowering his head when he said, 'What about the trails from here on up there, Sam?'

Picket responded differently; he was back on safe ground again. 'From here, they can't see the wagon. Not even if they move camp away from their meadow. We got several choices; there's game trails all up through there, and mostly, they will take a man to decent feed and good water.' Anticipating someone else's next question, he also said, 'We'd ought to be able to ride into their meadow before noon tomorrow, if we head out early enough.' Sam then looked in Dick's direction. This was Dick Chase's undertaking, and there was going to be unpleasantness if he and his crew found men in that upland meadow branding Chase cattle.

Dick stubbed out his smoke before speaking. 'Can you take us up around the top of that meadow, Sam? We'd be better off if we could get clear of any watchers they might have. We don't want a war, we just want to catch them with brandin' irons in their hands.'

Picket frowned in hard thought, and

24

eventually said, 'Yeah; I can get you above the meadow. But it'll take more time.'

Dick studied Sam's features. 'Then we'd better roll out and get to riding a long time before sunrise, hadn't we?'

Sam agreed by nodding his head. Gus Hanson groaned, then heaved up to his feet and without a word to anyone, went shuffling away in search of his bedroll. That amused Frank too. He watched the bear-like shadow of Gus briefly, then wagged his head over something which still intrigued him, even after having ridden with Gus for months. How did a man who was built like a bear, manage to be co-ordinated and even graceful, on a saddle animal?

Gus's precedent, plus Dick's remark about being in the saddle very early, put them all in mind of bedding down. Sam went out to look at the horses. He was not particularly concerned about varmints because the noise, movement and scent of men up in that high meadow would have fairly well routed all the big wild animals; what Sam wanted to be certain of was that the hobbles were all in place. When he returned Dick was standing over beside the war-wagon. He looked around to ask if everything was all right.

'Good enough,' stated Picket, and strolled over to say, 'What about Dan Corbett?'

'Maybe in the morning,' replied Dick. 'If we didn't see any sign of him on our way out, he

25

likely didn't get away from town very early, and maybe he won't even get away before morning.'

Sam found the hole in that logic. 'You told Dan you thought it was Brackett?'

Dick nodded. 'Yes. He got a little fired up with indignation. I guessed they were old friends.'

'That'd be all the more reason for him to be out here tonight, not in the morning,' stated Sam Picket. 'And yeah, I guess they're friends—but mainly I'd guess he'd want to stop a lynching.'

This did not seem to interest Dick. He leaned on the oak wagon-side gazing at Picket. 'I've only talked to Corbett twice. He seemed to be as good at his trade as he has to be.'

Sam returned his employer's steady regard. 'He's getting' a little age on him for long rides any more, or maybe it's got less to do with age than with settin' on his butt in town most of the time, and gettin' punky and a little fat, but he's not a man to play favourites . . . I've seen him a time or two at the bar in town with Barney Brackett. If you're wonderin' whether he'd side with Barney in something like this, Dick, I'd bet a new hat he wouldn't. Goin' after Brackett would embarrass hell out of him, make him feel awful and all—but he'd still go after him.'

Dick softly smiled in the starlight. 'That's good enough for me. I sort of had him figured out that way, Sam, but, like I've been saying, I'm new to the country.'

They parted, Dick to bed down beneath the war-wagon, Sam to go farther out, nearer the area where the horses were so that if anything occurred out there he would be awakened by the sounds. Sam was a light sleeper and always had been, which was something he considered about equal parts a blessing and a curse.

Gus snored. Even away under the wagon Dick heard it, and heaved up onto his opposite side so he would not have to hear it.

Autumn was still distant; even the softwood trees had not begun to show the withering reds and russets which would presage the end of summer and the beginning of fall, but there was an early chill in the night air to indicate the wait for autumn might not be as prolonged this year as it was some years.

The stars were like transparent crystal with flickering light behind them, and although the moon was little more than a curving sickle, it added a little light. Not enough, even with stars, to make visibility very good though.

And the cold increased as the night wore along. It did not bother men curled into bedrolls with coats for pillows, but it was out there waiting to ambush them when they rolled out in the dark and groped for boots, hats, shellbelts and guns. It struck into their warmed bodies to the marrow. They shrugged into their coats, which helped, and Gus

27

Hanson fumbled for a muffler he almost always wore in cold weather. Evidently his beard did not do the job Mother Nature had designed it for; at least it did not do it as well as a thick muffler did.

They left the team-horses out beyond the wagon, left their blanket-rolls and provisions, saddled up with just their Winchesters booted into place as extra baggage, then without speaking, followed Sam Picket as he aimed dead ahead for the timbered mountains. They were all thinking some variation of the identical idea; why in hell would anyone who had the same sense gawd gave a prairie dog, ever follow range-riding as a profession? Back down there in Butterfield even the livery barn swamper was warm in his blankets, even the barman and the blacksmith were going eventually to roll out when the sun came, and sit down to a hot meal and fresh coffee, in a warm kitchen.

They rode hunched inside their coats, unmindful of much except the bobbing man ahead a few yards; and when the land began to tilt sharply, and the good scent of pine and fir sap came up around them, they noticed that a lot less than they noticed how damned dark it was in among the big trees, and how treacherous the bone-dry, greasy-seeming pine needles were underfoot.

But at Dutra ranch they never shod horses without caulks in the rear, unless they were shoeing exclusively for roping, in which case, they used flat plates; but these animals had been re-shod a month back when there had been little reason for using plates. They had been re-shod with caulks so that they would have the best possible digging-in power, as well as easing the load on tendons. There were blessed few working horses in this world which did not benefit from caulks behind.

Dick was in the rear. He could not see Sam up ahead, partly because of the worse darkness among the big old trees, and partly because Gus was directly behind Sam, and with a coat on his broad, thick back, it would have been almost impossible to see two men ahead of Gus, let alone one man.

They picked up the scent of smoke after they had been in the saddle a couple of hours. Dick thought it was coming from the west. He also thought it was stale smoke, probably the residue from the burned-down campfire they had seen the day before.

Sam did not slacken off except to give the horses a chance to blow a couple of times. He rode up some trails, and crossed over other trails. He was riding by instinct in the right direction, but he was a knowledgeable horseman, he never made a direct bee-line if the slope was steep. These were the only horses they had, up in here.

The smell of smoke came and went. There was no air stirring, so that smoke had to be a

29

fair distance to their left; they were riding upon the perimeter of its greatest reach. Dick was satisfied about that.

Then a dove-coloured sky showed in the rare places where they could see through treetops. They were well up into the mountains by this time, so if the men they were seeking put out a watcher after they rolled out and ate, by which time it would be daylight, or at least very close to daylight, the watcher would see nothing but the endless miles of open country. Unless of course he scouted eastward a couple of miles and saw fresh shod-horse tracks, but Dick was not very worried about that happening.

Sam halted on a wide ledge, got down and stretched while his horse rested, then walked back to Dick and said, 'My guess is that we're maybe two, three miles east and north of that meadow . . . You want to leave the horses and stalk down there on foot?'

'When we're close enough,' Dick replied. 'Scout up the meadow for us. We'll wait back with the horses. What you see will determine what we do—on foot or on horseback.'

Sam went back, swung up and rode in the new direction until he found an elk trail—it was too wide at the top to have been made by anything else—and here, as they went ploddingly along over level ground, the scent of smoke was more noticeable. In fact it was with them all the time.

30

Sam halted near a brawling little white-water creek with water so cold it hurt a man's teeth. He took his carbine and struck out on foot. Dick, Gus, Frank and Jim stepped down to work kinks out of their legs and to give a rest to the backs of their animals. No one offered to roll a smoke, although under different circumstances they might have; smoke was a poor substitute for breakfast, but to some men it was better than just standing around sucking air.

Frank shifted his holstered Colt and freed the tie-down. He considered Gus's dour, whiskery face and said, 'You should have stayed with bein' a town carpenter.'

Gus's small, sunk-set eyes brightened with irony. 'Sure. Except that a man can't eat wood, and when times get bad nobody needs windows or doors or even pine coffins.' Gus looked at them all, slowly, then added a little more in his deep, rumbly, slow-spaced voice. 'And a man misses all this; them beautiful big old trees, the sweet-smellin' invigoratin' air, half-frozen feet, a sore butt and an empty belly.'

Jim grinned.

Dick's eyes twinkled at Gus. Like the other riders, he was intrigued by Hanson's ability to ride, rope, and do all the myriad other chores rangemen had to perform almost every day, and do them all as though he weighed a hundred and sixty pounds instead of more than two hundred pounds.

'Missin' breakfast might be good for you,' he said, and Gus turned his villainously bearded face to gaze expressionlessly at his employer for a moment before answering.

'Maybe. I've done it a lot in my lifetime. But what's good for a man an' what he likes damned rarely are the same thing.'

Frank chuckled, then they all turned at a slight sound up in front of the horses. Sam was back, carbine in the bend of one arm.

CHAPTER FOUR

THE MOUNTAIN MEADOW COUNTRY

Sam squatted, picked up a twig and began sketching in the trail-dust. He created an uneven but roughly oblong drawing. 'They're down by a fire-ring, four of 'em, but out where the horses are, there are six animals. Maybe the other two men are out in the woods, or maybe those are pack horses. I couldn't get close enough to make certain.'

Sam raised his eyes to Dick Chase. 'They got pole corrals, looks like maybe four of 'em, and they got about two hundred head of short yearlings in there, just like it was before, except that the corrals wasn't built and there weren't any men up here. But it's our cattle

32

sure as I'm sitting here.'

Dick nodded because he had not doubted any of this, even though he'd had no idea there would be new corrals up here. 'What about the men?' he asked, and Sam leaned to poke in the dirt with his stick.

'This is where they got their camp gear. It's scattered around but the grass is too tall to be able to make it out very well from a distance.'

Sam paused to straighten up slightly. 'But I could make out saddleboots and Winchesters.'

Frank, still concerned about the number of men in the meadow, said, 'How many Winchesters, Sam?'

'I don't know. I couldn't see down there very well, but I saw about three of them.' Having disposed of that Sam leaned to make another hole in the dust. 'This is where they been working the cattle. They're over there now, stirrin' up the fire again.' He tossed the twig away. 'Dick, they're just about in the middle of that meadow.'

Picket did not explain why that was significant. He did not have to. Gus Hanson said, 'How tall's the grass?'

Sam smiled a little. 'Not tall enough to hide you, Gus. Maybe the rest of us could belly-crawl through it, but not you.'

If that troubled Hanson he gave no indication of it; he simply leaned, looking at Picket's diagram with his old saddlegun drooping, and eventually came up with something the others found useful.

'All right. You fellers crawl and I'll stand back, an' if they see you too soon, I'll get their damned attention.'

Dick ignored them all and studied the diagram until he was satisfied, then he stood up and said, 'How close can we get?'

Sam also arose. 'Half a mile closer.'

They left this place on horseback, riding slowly now and watching for Sam's upraised arm. When it came they were among enormous black-trunked fir trees whose lowest limbs looked to be easily sixty feet from the forest floor. Tying the horses was not as difficult as this might have made it appear to be. There were innumerable twenty-foot seedlings growing at random.

Dick shed his coat. It was not warm yet, at least it was not yet warm in the forest although out in open country it was warm enough. It would probably never be satisfactorily warm where they rolled and tied their coats, but it was not really cold either.

Sam led the way. He used a narrow game-trail for about two-thirds of the distance, then slanted downhill where there was no trail. Fortunately, neither was there underbrush. They stopped where Sam halted to wait. This, he told Frank and Jim, was where he had spied upon the meadow. Then he worked still lower and led them into a small clearing. From this point of vantage they had an excellent sighting of the meadow.

It was perhaps forty or fifty acres in size, the grass was grazed over but still almost stirrup-high. Like most mountain meadows this one appeared to be fed by abundant underground reserves of snow-water. It was a beautiful place, surrounded as it was by immense, black-barked trees. Sunlight came down into the meadow, making a stark contrast with the surrounding forest gloom.

Dick knelt, leaned upon his carbine, did not particularly notice the meadow itself, and watched four men moving about near the green-pole corrals. A fifth man appeared with an armload of dry wood and dumped his burden beside the small fire. Dick leaned to speak to Frank Longtree. 'How good are your eyes, Frank?'

'Why?'

'Because I think they got branding irons slanting out of the fire.'

'They do have,' replied Longtree, looking around.

'And that means they probably aren't using running irons, don't it?'

'Brackett's irons . . .'

Frank turned back toward the distant working area without speaking.

Sam came down and squatted near Dick Chase. 'We can get a hell of a lot closer from up at this side of the opening. Through the grass. They're not goin' to notice us anyway,

35

they got their hands full.'

Gus was scowling at the distant scene of activity. 'Four, five men to mark two hunnert short yearlings . . .' He looked at Sam. 'How long they been up here? Hell, five men had ought to be able to get this done in a couple days.'

Picket's reply was practical. 'They built those pole corrals, Gus. That'd take 'em three, four days.'

Jim Jones was anxious to move. He gestured with an outflung arm. 'We can get as close as we want. Let's go.

Dick did not move, and until he moved or agreed that his riders should move, no one was going to start ahead. He studied the men, listened to the wild bawl of a roped animal down by the fire, and finally nodded his head.

Dick left the trees first, on his all-fours pushing the carbine ahead the way the oldtime stalking redskins had done it. The distance was considerable, the grass was tall enough to mask their advance, and now that they were out in sunlight it was warm enough; if they had not shed their coats it would have been too warm.

Gus remained near the final rank of trees. Dick paused a couple of times looking back, but Gus was not discernible among all the other gloomy shapes and shadows back yonder.

When he was mid-way toward the corrals

with the stench of burnt hair and hide in the smoke which was rolling outward from the corral-area, he sank lower and looked for the others.

Frank and Jim Jones were nearly side by side. Jim exposed his head more often than Frank did. Jim also seemed anxious to get up ahead. Frank had to growl at him several times. Dick looked over where Sam Picket was. Sam may have done this before, but whether that was true or not, he certainly moved as though he knew about stalking. When he slipped ahead not even the grass swayed and when he sank down, he was invisible.

Dick shoved forward again. He had his gloves on so his hands did not suffer much from contact with thorny weeds in the lush grass, but his knees got tender, making him flinch each time he came down upon a sharp pebble.

They could hear men calling back and forth at the corrals or at the fire. They could also hear explosive curses, and much less often, someone's voice raised in a tough laugh.

Dick stopped again. They were within carbine range now. It would have been easy to raise up, aim, and shoot down all five of those unsuspecting men. Dick shook sweat off his nose and chin, wondered why they hadn't had a watcher out, and began inching ahead again, his bruised knees becoming sensitive now, even to grass clumps, which were tough, fibrous and spiny.

The grazing horses were off a fair distance on Dick's and Sam's left, but they picked up the scent and almost simultaneously flung up their heads and whirled around to come to a poised, stiff halt, staring.

For a long time the working men at the branding fire noticed nothing. Dick cursed the horses; ordinarily, horses would not have held that spooked stance so long, they would have lost interest when no danger appeared, and would have resumed grazing. These animals did no such thing, and Dick heard a man cry out above the slavering noise a hog-tied big calf was making as a man advanced upon him with a hot iron. The man with the iron stopped and turned. The man on the ground with the big calf also twisted to peer out at the horses.

Finally, the lanky man with the branding iron turned completely around, looking intently in the same direction the horses were staring. His iron was cooling very fast and would have to be re-heated now.

Dick had grass before his eyes as he intently watched. Sam was invisible on Dick's left, to his right Frank and Jim were scarcely visible to Dick and were not visible at all to the men at the branding fire, all of whom had now got to their feet and were staring. Someone's sharp voice distinctly said: 'Damned bear. Likely the same one that was around here last night spookin' the horses . . . Ham, take your carbine and run that son of a bitch out of here.'

A short man with sloping, heavy shoulders pulled off his gloves as he walked over where the camp equipment was scattered, yanked a saddlegun from its scabbard, and began walking on a diagonal course toward the hidden men, lugging his Winchester in one fist as though he did not intend to use it as anything but a club.

Dick reached high, parted the grass very gently, and looked out there. The man called Ham was wearing faded, stained and shiny old shotgun chaps. It was not Ham that worried Dick, it was the other four men. They had cover down there by those corrals. Dick and his men had no cover at all except tall grass, and it was not noted for deflecting ground-sluicing bullets.

He placed his saddlegun to one side, drew his Colt, rocked back slightly to get weight off his sore knees, and waited. They were too far from the trees to race back there for protection, and if they ran in the opposite direction they were going to be riddled by the cattle thieves up at the fire.

Someone on Dick's left made a rattling sound in the grass. Frank Longtree was scuttling away from Jim Jones toward Dick. It was a foolish thing to do with an armed man bearing down on them, but evidently Ham was too distant to see the moving grass-heads.

39

Frank reached his employer, sank flat and gestured savagely with his free hand toward his back, toward the direction from which he had been crawling. In a tight, excited whisper, he said, 'A rider. Look southeastward. There's a horseman workin' back and forth through the trees over there!'

Dick continued to watch Ham, and only spared a couple of seconds to glance in this new direction. He saw nothing, no horse and rider, no movement of any kind.

From down by the pole corrals a man sang out. 'Ham! Come on back!'

Dick could not believe it. Two men walked out a ways and used big looping arm gestures to summon Ham back to the corrals. Then, finally, Dick saw the horseman Frank had been so excited about. He was riding into the sunlight toward the corrals. Everyone could have seen him now, and evidently the men at the corrals had not only seen him but had recognised him because they started toward the east side of their working area; and there they stopped and stood expectantly, as though the horseman was someone they had not only been expecting, but someone they wanted to talk to.

Dick raised a soiled sleeve to mop greasy sweat off. Frank was sitting on his haunches. So were Jim and Sam. They were all watching the stranger approach. Ham got back down there and joined his companions, still carrying

40

the saddlegun. All their backs were to the men in the tall grass. Sam came slightly closer and said, 'Who does that look like, Dick?'

Chase shook his head. He had been watching the newcomer for several minutes. It did not look like anyone he might know until Sam Picket said, 'Dan Corbett,' then Dick tried harder to make an identification.

When Sam said that name, Frank Livingstone swore in a surprised undertone. 'Sure as hell,' he said.

They said no more. Each one of them was occupied with his busy thoughts. Those rustlers were clustered close as the rider came up to them, stopped and leaned on his saddlehorn to speak. The distant men in the grass could not make out even the sounds of conversation, but what troubled them much more was the easy way Corbett, if indeed that *was* the marshal from Butterfield, was entirely at ease, and the rustlers were the same way.

Dick hissed and jerked his head in the direction from which they had come. Corbett knew Dick and his crew were up here somewhere. Whether he suspected they were close or not, he would certainly start making a sashay directly, and if he found Dick with the others out here, on foot in the grass . . .

They went back much faster than they had crawled forward. Even so it required almost an hour before they could see Gus leaning on a big tree, watching their approach, and also

41

looking down where that horseman had dismounted and was leading his horse over among the corrals.

Jim got back first. He stood up with grass-stain on his knees and gloves, told Gus what they had seen, and Hanson looked incredulous. He peered intently, but the distance was far too great, so when Sam and Frank and Dick came up, he said, 'If he's figurin' on arresting five of them by himself, he's crazy.'

Dick's legs ached. Sam's probably did also but Sam was feeling in pockets for his plug and looking slit-eyed back down toward the pole corrals. As he was skiving off a fresh cud he said, 'We better ride back on there, stayin' back in the trees . . . But Gus, it didn't look to me like Dan Corbett was tryin' to arrest anyone.'

It was a long hike to the horses, but at least it could be made while they were standing erect, and when they reached the animals, which had been dozing comfortably, and swung up over leather, Dick said, 'I got a feeling that something is goin' on.'

Jim looked around. 'Somethin' like what?'

Dick wagged his head. 'I don't know. It's just a feeling.'

Gus growled. 'Yeah; somethin' is goin' on if Dan Corbett is friendly to a set of cattle thieves.'

Dick took the lead. Directly behind him Gus

Hanson plodded along as he had done behind Sam Picket on the way up here, and when Dick twisted to see if they were all coming, he had to rein clear of Gus to make sure.

Nothing was said. Sam and Frank looked puzzled and uneasy. Gus looked grim and bleak. Jim Jones, who was like a goose and awakened in a new world every morning, showed nothing on his face but strong curiosity.

CHAPTER FIVE

OUT OF THE MOUNTAINS

Sam Picket may have been particularly troubled about Marshal Corbett's appearance, and the way he had met with the cattle thieves, because Sam had defended Dan Corbett to Dick; but the other rangemen appeared not to be inhibited toward Corbett at all. They did not speak much on the ride down through the firs, but Gus said, 'We'd ought to hang that son of a bitch too,' when Dick looked back, and this seemed to be the feeling of both Jim Jones and Frank Longtree.

When they were roughly parallel to the cow-camp on their right, over in the centre of that beautiful meadow, they dismounted, led the horses off a short distance, left them and returned, carrying carbines.

Frank found fresh shod-horse sign. It was Corbett's, and it seemed to come directly up-country as though the lawman had ridden along the base of the foothills until he knew he was below the meadow. Then he had ridden directly up there. Dick wondered if he had found the war-wagon. It was not very likely, unless Corbett had sashayed back and forth through the foothills, and Dick's guess was that he had not; that he had been in a hurry and had ridden along the flat land out front of the hills.

Jim slipped as close as the foremost stand of trees, and stood in shadows down there watching the men at the cow-camp. Dick and Sam palavered farther back. Dick was of the opinion that Corbett would say that he had ridden up here to convey a message, then head back on his way home. He told Sam they had plenty of time; they could simply sit down and wait, then nail Dan Corbett when he rode out of the meadow and into the forest.

Sam was agreeable but Gus wondered whether Corbett would, in fact, actually ride back this way. Dick shrugged. 'If he don't, we'll trail him and overhaul him.'

Gus's worry proved groundless. Jim came hurrying back to report that Marshal Corbett was beside his horse tightening the *cincha,* and talking to a faded-looking man with greying hair.

Sam Picket did not look very pleased, but when Dick nodded at Jim and sent him back to keep watch, then turned and said, 'We'll just stop him and have a little talk,' Picket was agreeable. Gloomily so, but agreeable.

They could see Corbett when he rode away from the pole corrals. He was indeed following the same route out of the meadow that he had used to enter it. Jim came back, slyly smiling.

Dick leaned against a big tree with his carbine-carrying men around him in similar stances. They all watched Marshal Corbett ride toward them in bright sunlight. He was relaxed and easy in the saddle, and his sorrel horse moved along as though he were entirely at peace with the world too.

Dick shook his head. He knew what he had seen, knew what interpretation other men would have put on it, and yet in the back of his mind he had an uneasy feeling that there was something about all this that was not going to turn out as he had expected.

He turned toward Sam Picket. Sam was faintly frowning, his rugged countenance set in an expression of pained censure.

Gus and Frank were opposite the site where Corbett would leave the meadow and enter the forest. Each of them had his carbine in both hands. A man with a saddlegun could not be as quick at using it as a man with a sixgun— unless the man with the sixgun was taken completely by surprise, and this, Frank and

Gus were confident, was about to happen.

It did. Dan Corbett ducked around a thick-boled fir tree, the sunlight left him, shadows mantled his shoulders—and he saw Gus Hanson first, then Frank Longtree, and as his horse moved ahead a yard or two before Corbett lifted his rein-hand, he also saw Sam, Dick and Jim. He stopped stone-still.

Dick said, 'Get down, Marshal, and keep both hands in sight.'

He had not raised his voice. Corbett obeyed, stepped ahead of his horse trailing both reins, and as his surprised expression began to fade, a tougher look firmed up. He said, 'I came by the ranch, Mister Chase. You'd already left.'

Dick ignored that. 'What were you doing out there just now, Marshal?'

Corbett shifted his stance, let all his considerable heft rest upon one leg, and answered curtly. 'I was carryin' a message from John Singletary, Brackett's rangeboss. I met Singletary below the foothills. We had a long talk.' Corbett looked at each one of them before continuing. Evidently what he had to say was going to take time. He looked back at Dick and spoke again.

'Those aren't your cattle, Mister Chase. They're heifers that Brackett did not want down on the range where the bulls would breed them too young.'

Chase and his men understood at least part

46

of that statement. No cowman who intended to keep quality heifers for replacement, wanted them bred before they were at least two years old, but in open range country where bulls roamed at will—and by scent—it was impossible to do this unless the heifers were isolated, either in corrals or a long distance from the bulls. What they did not understand was what prompted Gus to say, 'Marshal, I seen those critters up close. I recognised three of 'em that has unusual markings. They came off Dutra cows. I saw 'em as baby calves, and I saw 'em up here on the meadow.'

Corbett gazed steadily at Gus for a moment before speaking. 'You got to be mistaken. John Singletary told me he cut out those animals himself, selected them as replacement heifers for their quality. He said he knew every damned one them by sight.' Corbett waited, but Gus simply stood staring back, so Corbett also said, 'Mister Chase, I'm relieved as hell that you didn't make trouble. That worried me all the way from town. Now then—I got no idea how this all come about, how this mistake got made, but I've known Mister Brackett and his rangeboss a long time, and when they explain things to me, I got to accept what they say unless someone else can convince me they're lying.'

Sam Picket spoke for the first time. 'Dan; Singletary's wrong.'

Corbett shot back a sharp answer. 'Prove it,

47

Sam!'

Gus growled. 'I just did.'

Corbett turned on him. 'No, you didn't. You said you recognised some calves. Mister, we got maybe as many as sixteen, maybe eighteen, thousand head of cattle in the Tenino basin. They're every colour under the sun and they come speckled, brockle-faced, spotted, off-colour an' full-colour. You could find the same markings somewhere in the basin on other cattle.'

Gus was a dogged man, and a short-tempered one as well. He stood regarding the other large man for a while, then said, 'Marshal, I know what I'm talkin' about. But even if I didn't an' if you been around livestock at all, will you tell me why Mister Brackett let them big heifers go this long without branding them?'

Corbett was getting a little red in the face. 'That's up to him, cowboy. Other stockmen have done the same thing. Whatever their reason, it's their business.'

Dick, sensing trouble coming, broke in. 'Ride down with us, Marshal. I'd like to talk to Mister Brackett.'

Corbett shrugged. 'You'll have to talk to his rangeboss, Barney's over in Denver to see an eye-doctor.'

Dick was agreeable. 'Fine. You lead the way and we'll palaver with the rangeboss.'

Dan Corbett mounted, looked openly

48

hostile as he glanced around, then reined southward down through the trees. Behind him Gus Hanson got directly behind, and the last two riders in the queue were Frank Singleton and Dick Chase. Frank rode several hundred yards before quietly saying, 'I think you're right, there is somethin' goin' on . . . when I was headin' home yesterday from over this way lookin' for strays and cut-backs, I saw Brackett and his rangeboss riding southward, as though they might have been up in the foothills a mile or two east of where we left the war-wagon.

Dick rolled and lit a smoke. 'Maybe Brackett left for Denver this morning, Frank.'

Longtree answered with doubt in his voice. 'Maybe.'

When they reached open country and could close up a little, Dan Corbett sought out Sam Picket and rode aside with him as they conversed. The other rangemen left them alone, but Gus Hanson was like a troublesome mastiff, he looked back from time to time as though he did not trust Corbett to remain with them.

It was a long ride on empty stomachs. Their camp-equipment and grub was back at the war-wagon. Dick had considered sending Gus back for it. The reason he did not do this was because he did not know whether to tell Gus to drive the wagon toward Brackett's home-place, or back to his own.

It was not very critical in any case; someone could always go back for the wagon.

Frank said, 'You never met John Singletary?'

Dick hadn't; in fact he had never met anyone from the adjoining range. He had thought of riding over and introducing himself when he had a little more time, perhaps when the first frost arrived.

'He's a tough man,' stated Longtree. 'He's been with Mister Brackett maybe a year now, or maybe a little less. He don't like riders from other outfits on their range. And he hired a new crew when he become foreman. In some ways him and Mister Brackett are alike.'

'In what ways?' Dick asked out of curiosity.

'Well; they're both long-legged, rawhide sort of men. And they don't neither of them go out of their way to be neighbourly, which is all right I guess, but most range stockmen aren't that way. In open range country the day'll come when you got to have help from a neighbour.'

Dick was looking ahead, half-listening to Frank's generalisations, when he made out rooftops in a setting of old trees about two miles ahead. The closer they got to the set of buildings the more rugged and functional they looked. By the time they were approaching the yard Dick's opinion was that Brackett too, had been in the Tenino basin a long time, maybe almost as long as Dick's uncle had been there.

50

He wished his uncle could have been along. At least he would have been able to guide his nephew in what lay ahead. As it now was, Dick was entirely on his own, and up ahead Dan Corbett was distinctly hostile. As for the story Corbett had told them back up in the big timber—it could be true. Unlikely, but true. But whether it was or not, Dick was still short a couple of hundred head, and since bears, wolves and cougars had certainly not eaten that many, and they had not sprouted wings and flown away, why then, there was someone, somewhere, who had an explanation; and if Dick had not believed what he had seen and what his men had said, he would not have been out here today.

Right now, what it appeared to boil down to, was the word of his men who had recognised those long yearlings as having been small calves on his cows, and the word of Barney Brackett's rangeboss.

He already knew who Marshal Corbett believed. They were entering the big, shady yard from the northeast when a lanky man sauntered down off the cook-house porch, crossed to the front of the log barn, and leaned on a tie-rack over there, waiting.

Sam eased back to ride stirrup with Dick, and Marshal Corbett pushed up ahead. Sam said, 'He thinks you went off half-cocked. He told me before you got all fired up you should have scoured our range, then looked

51

elsewhere. He said two hundred strays out of four or five thousand critters isn't uncommon.

Dick nodded about that. 'Strays, no, that wouldn't be uncommon, but critters that disappeared, that would be uncommon.'

'Yeah. Well; that's why he said you should have made more of an effort to find the darned things.'

They were crossing toward that lanky man in front of the barn. Dan Corbett swung off first, spoke briefly to the lanky man; then, as the other riders stopped and dismounted, Corbett gestured toward Dick Chase and introduced him to John Singletary, the lanky, hard-faced rangeboss of Barney Brackett, whose small, perpetually-squinted eyes considered Dick shrewdly as Singletary gravely nodded, then said, 'Dan told me you was out some cattle.'

Dick walked slowly forward and halted a yard away nodding his head and holding both reins in his gloved hands as he too made a judgment. John Singletary looked hard, knowledgeable, and politely unfriendly.

'Did you find them, Mister Chase?' the rangeboss asked, his eyes as still as stones.

Gus Hanson, with oaken arms crossed over his massive chest, growled an answer. 'We found 'em. Up yonder in that meadow where your crew is—'

'You saw *some cattle*,' snapped Marshal Corbett, whose position was not enviable. It was very dangerous to ride into a man's yard and say anything at all that might be construed as calling him a cattle-thief. Dan Corbett had made up his mind long before they got down here, that he was not going to permit a fight to start. The last thing he needed this late in the working season was a killing. He did not need one any time, but particularly now, with the riding season nearly over when most rangemen would be paid off and head south, would disperse so that feuds would have to sputter out and die for lack of men to keep them alive.

John Singletary made his appraisal of Gus Hanson, gazed at Frank and Jim and Sam Picket, then turned back toward Dick and said, 'You'll find them, Mister Chase. In fact, we've turned back at least that many of your strays over on our range this summer.'

Sam coloured. That was a slur. Every outfit had strays during the grazing season, but no outfit which was operated the way Dutra and his nephew ran the Dutra place, did not hunt down and bring back its strays. But Sam said nothing. He was a little like Dan Corbett in this affair; he did not want a fight to start. At least not now when there had been doubts cast upon the validity of what he and his campanions had been doing up in the mountains.

Gus Hanson was willing though. He replied to Singletary's slur with a growled response. 'What was you doin', Mister Singletary—

53

lookin' for more big quality heifers?'

That was fight talk. Singletary began slowly to pull up off the tie-rack when Dan Corbett swore with fierce feeling. 'Gawddammit, there's not goin' to be any more of that!' He glared at Gus, then turned on Dick Chase. 'Have you scoured the other ranges?'

Dick was gazing stonily at John Singletary. He had taken a firm dislike to the man. 'We looked around a little,' he replied, without taking his gaze off Brackett's rangeboss.

'A little?' exclaimed Corbett. 'You got any idea how many cattle there are an' how big Tenino basin is? Mister Chase; I said it before. You got to produce proof!'

Dick sighed and turned toward his horse. Without another word he swung up. His men followed that example. He led there at a slow walk out of the yard. Behind, where Singletary and Corbett stood, the rangeboss with the red, wrinkled neck watched his departing neighbours when he said, 'Marshal; if he lost two hundred head like he claims he did, and didn't look no farther than our range, he's either a greenhorn cowman, a damned fool— or a trouble-hunter.'

CHAPTER SIX

SOMETHING TO THINK ABOUT

They were several miles out when Dick said, 'Gus, take Jim and go fetch our wagon home.'

Hanson turned, jerked his head at Jones, and loped off in a different direction. Sam watched Gus leave, and wagged his head. 'That darned fool wouldn't take a step backwards if he was facin' a grizzly bear.'

Frank Longtree rode in glum silence. It seerned to him that his boss had been humiliated back there in Brackett's yard, and that rankled with Frank. They were well along when he finally said, 'Dick; you didn't have to take nothin' off that son of a bitch.'

Sam looked at his horse's ears as though he had not heard. Dick turned toward Frank. 'I didn't take anything off him, Frank.'

'Well hell, we rode out of the yard leavin' him to leave the last word.'

Dick poked along a short distance before speaking again. 'Frank, did you see that saddle hanging from a peg just inside the barn doorway?'

This time Sam turned, as did Frank, but Frank's expression showed candid bafflement. 'Yeah, I saw it.'

'And did you look in their wagon shed?'

This was too much. 'Their wagon shed . . .! What the hell's that got to do with us riding out like we had our tails tucked between our legs?'

'I'll tell you,' stated Dick, looping reins and digging for his tobacco sack. 'Did you see the carved initials on the back of the cantle of that hangin' saddle? B.B.'

Frank exasperatedly said, 'Barney Brackett; for Chris'sake, he owns the place.'

Dick ignored the rasp in Longtree's voice. 'Did you hear Corbett tell us up yonder in the timber when we stopped him outside the meadow, that Singletary told him Brackett had gone over to Denver to have his eyes examined?'

'Yes, I heard him say that,' exclaimed the rangerider.

'Frank; if you lived this far from town where you'd take a stage to Denver, would you ride all that distance bareback?'

Frank did not reply. He and Sam were gazing steadily at Dick.

'Well, let's say you hurt your leg or your foot, or just plain didn't want to ride over there. Would you *walk*? No, you'd fit out one of those rigs which were in the shed and *drive* over there—only there was one topbuggy, the other rigs were wagons. You wouldn't drive a wagon, Frank, you'd take the buggy . . . It was covered with dust, even on the shafts. No one's used that buggy in a hell of a long time.'

Longtree's gaze wavered, slid to Sam Picket, then settled far ahead as his horse plodded along through the pleasant heat. It was Sam who finally said, 'Dick, the seatin' leather on that saddle was shiny. It'd been ridden real recent.'

Dick acknowledged that. 'Yeah . . . Frank told me he'd seen Brackett yesterday afternoon.'

Longtree acknowledged this with a nod in Sam's direction. 'Brackett and that rangeboss of his. Looked like maybe they was comin' down out of the foothills.'

Dick added a little more. 'Brackett was around yesterday afternoon. Frank saw him. That would account for his saddle-seat still lookin' shiny . . . What's sticking in my craw is that if he was around yesterday, fine; then maybe he left for Denver this morning—but the way Marshal Corbett said it back up in the mountains was that Brackett was already gone, and *had* been gone for a spell . . . But he didn't take a rig to town and leave it like most folks do so's he'd have something to drive home in when he returned, and he didn't take his saddle.'

Sam rummaged for his cut plug, saying nothing. Frank rode a fair distance and did not speak either. Around them the day was fading out. There would still be hours of light left, but they were on the sundown side of it now, as they booted their mounts over into a lope and held them to it for about fifteen minutes, then Sam hauled back down to a walk, spat aside, shifted in the saddle looking sceptically at Dick.

'What you got in mind?' he asked.

Dick looked troubled but not upset. 'I don't know, Sam.'

'You think someone lied about Barney being gone?'

'It looks that way, Sam,'

'Oh for Chris'sake, spit it out, Dick.'

Chase regarded his companions steadily and without speaking for a long time, then he eventually said. 'All right. If Brackett was a cattle thief, my uncle would have known it, and probably would have buried Brackett. That's bothered me right from the start. Now then— where is Barney Brackett? Sure as hell he didn't *drive* away, and sure as hell he didn't *ride* away—so where is he?' Neither Frank nor Sam attempted to answer. Probably Chase had not intended for them to because he immediately said, 'Singletary's running things. It was Singletary sent those men up to the pole-corral meadow to work the cattle, and it was Singletary who met Corbett and told him Brackett had gone to Denver. It was Singletary who looked me straight in the eye and lied about those long yearlings.'

Frank suddenly stiffened in his saddle. 'Gawda'mighty,' he exclaimed, then hesitated as though unwilling to say the rest of it.

58

But Sam had a lot less compunction. 'Brackett's—dead?'

Dick considered the flopping mane of his horse without speaking for a while, then he said, 'Tell you what let's do—let's head for that swale yonder with the creek-willows in it, and get down and rest a little.'

Sam did not have the answer he had sought, and, as with Frank Longtree a half hour earlier, he failed to see any connection between his question and what his employer had just said, so he first frowned in the direction of the willow-thicket swale, then he frowned in Chase's direction and said, 'What the hell for; you tired?'

'No. But Marshal Corbett'll be along directly. We can waylay him, set him down and have a real long talk with him.'

Sam was still scowling as he turned back to look at the distant swale, but at least this time he did not look as though the idea did not appeal to him.

It required another half-hour to reach the swale, go down its west slope to the wide, grassy bottom, and on over to the willows where there had been water earlier in the summer but where there was nothing but mud now, and many birds whose angry denunciation of this trespass shrilled up and down the length of the swale.

They loosened their saddles, draped bridles from saddlehorns, hobbled their horses and let them graze. Sam whittled off a fresh chew and Sam Longtree sat cross-legged like an old buck Indian and meticulously rolled a smoke, something he invariably did with great care when he was bothered by some thought. When he had lit up he glanced over where Dick Chase was watching the horses, and said, 'How long you reckon it's been goin' on?'

Dick turned with a shrug. 'Maybe it isn't, Frank . . . It's just that Singletary was too damned possessive. But maybe that's his manner. I don't know him that well.'

Frank got disgusted. 'Dick, if you figured all that out, sure as hell you believe it . . . What I'd like to know is, how long's it been goin' on, and where is Barney Brackett?'

Sam was a forthright individual. Once he fastened upon an idea he was blunt in mentioning it. Now, after listening to Dick and Frank, he said, 'Barney's buried, that's where he is. Corbett won't believe it. He's pig-headed. But I'll bet a new hat Brackett's dead and buried.' Sam spat, something he rarely did when he had a fresh cud in his cheek. 'Now I'm beginning to understand something. Dick, you said this morning it didn't make sense for a big cowman like Brackett to steal a couple hundred head of long yearlings.'

Dick nodded, listening and saying nothing.

'He *didn't* steal 'em, Dick, that son of a bitch Singletary stole them. And I'll tell you something else; when Singletary took over as

60

Mister Brackett's rangeboss, he replaced all the riders with men *he* hired . . . Now what does that sound like to you?'

Dick answered quietly. 'Like a band of high-powered rustlers who have moved up to somethin' a hell of a lot more profitable than just stealin' a few head of cattle here and there.' Before Sam or Frank could say anything, Dick jutted his jaw toward the slope they had ridden down to reach their present resting place. 'Frank, ride up there and see if Mister Corbett's coming, will you?'

After Longtree loped away Dick regarded Sam Picket. 'I think you're right, Sam. I also think Singletary was a damned fool to covet two hundred long yearlings when he had all of Brackett's cattle to steal . . . And I also think he's been stealin' them, which would account for the fact that we haven't seen any Brackett critters all day.'

Sam sat down in the grass, put his hat beside him and absently pulled a grass stalk which he plugged between his lips. Eventually, when he looked up and saw Frank sitting on the skyline, he said, 'I never in my life heard of a rustler working like this, and I've heard of a lot of cattle thieves . . . But Dan Corbett won't believe it.' Sam added that last sentence with ringing conviction in his voice.

Dick did not comment, he too was watching Frank Longtree. Even if Marshal Corbett angled more southeasterly in a direct line for

61

Butterfield, Frank would see him from up there.

Dick sat down too, lay back and tipped his hat over his face. In a voice that sounded sepulchral from beneath the hat he said, 'I don't much care what Corbett believes. I just want him to listen, that's all. Just listen. He don't have to believe it, Sam, but it'll sure help if he'll get a little sceptical about John Singletary, and those men up in that meadow branding our cattle.'

Picket was already beyond considering the big lawman. 'We'll never find old Brackett, Dick. His range is as big as ours. And we'll *have* to find him. Corbett will demand that.'

The muffled voice sounded the same again. 'I think we can find him. Maybe it'll take a little lookin' but I think—'

'I just told you, Dick, Brackett's got thousands of acres and some of it's 'way up in those damned mountains.'

'Sam . . . Frank saw Brackett and his rangeboss yesterday afternoon up near the foothills . . . Today, Brackett isn't around.'

Sam Picket gave a start. 'Up there?'

'That'll be my guess. Frank can show us about where he saw them.'

A faint sound prompted Dick to lift his hat and raise his head. Frank was spinning his horse on the lip of the swale and gesturing with his hat.

Dick said, 'Let's get to riding, Sam. He's

seen Corbett.'

It required time to rig out and get astride. As they headed for the lip of the swale Frank got impatient, waved to them in the direction he was going to head out, and left the upper side of the swale in an easy lope, riding southward. When they got up there they could see Frank, and in the middle distance they could also see the marshal.

For a while Dan Corbett did not see three riders bearing down upon him from the northwest, and when he finally did notice them he rode a few yards, then stopped in his tracks and stared. He probably recognised them.

Frank reached Corbett first. He gestured and said, 'Dick wants to talk to you, Marshal.'

Corbett looked stonily back at Longtree. 'We've already talked. I want to get back to town before the café man locks up for the night.'

Frank smiled. 'You'd better listen.'

That probably did nothing to improve the big lawman's mood, because when Sam and Dick loped up he fixed them with a sour look. 'There's nothing more to say until you fellers come up with something better than the word of that rider of yours with the whiskers.'

Dan let his reins lie slack, relaxed in the saddle and began talking. The longer he talked the more incredulous became the expression on the lawman's face, and several times when Corbett was preparing to interrupt, Dick ignored this and went right on racking up his points. He did not say he *knew* any of this was true; all he did was place it all in good sequential order before the township marshal, and when he was finished, finally, he said, 'Marshal; like a lot of things in this life that happen to a man, I'm satisfied the parts I've told you are true; came from damned good sources. The rest of it I've strung together because it fits and *seems* to be true . . . All you got to do to make me look like a horse's rear end, is to show me Mister Brackett standin' up and breathing.'

Dan Corbett slid his gaze to Sam Picket, who was a friend, then back to Dick Chase again. He ignored Frank Longtree completely. 'How the hell can I produce Mister Brackett,' he growled, 'if he's in Denver?'

Dick accepted that. 'All right. Then tell me how he got there?'

'You mean the saddle and the buggy?'

'Yeah.'

For a while Corbett was silent, then his face brightened. 'He wouldn't ride it, so he'd take one of the stages out of Butterfield. They'll know at the stage office which stage he took.'

Dick accepted that also. 'And if they tell you he didn't take any of the stages to Denver?'

Corbett sat a little longer this time before answering. 'Why then I guess I'll have to come back out here and talk to Singletary.'

Dick considered the little ears of his horse

before drily answering that. 'If you do that, Marshal, you come by the ranch first, and I'll ride over there with you . . . If Singletary thinks there is only one man—you—gettin' suspicious, he's goin' to sock you away the same as he most likely did with Mister Brackett.'

Marshal Corbett coloured a little. 'If he tries it he'll get a hell of a surprise!'

Dick was not impressed. 'You alone out there, Marshal—him with his five riders.' Dick looked straight at the lawman. 'You got to come by the ranch anyway, to tell me that you found out that Mister Brackett went to Denver.'

Corbett considered the reddening sun. He still had a long ride—over ten miles—ahead of him. 'I'll stop by the ranch,' he grumbled, nodded just once and kneed his horse on its way.

CHAPTER SEVEN

BY STARLIGHT

By the time Sam and Frank were entering the yard with Dick Chase, Picket was ready to admit that Dick had presented a good case for his theory; good enough to impress Dan Corbett.

They put up the horses and went over to the cookshack to make a meal, and Frank Longtree was measuring coffee into the graniteware pot when he made an observation. 'If Corbett don't show up tomorrow it'll mean Brackett *did* take a stage out of Butterfield for Denver.'

Neither of the other men denied this, but Sam Picket, not as sceptical as he had been up until now, was nonetheless still looking for loopholes. 'It sticks in my craw how Corbett sided with Singletary over there today.'

Dick was frying meat and had to raise his voice to be heard when he said, 'I'm not so sure he was siding with Singletary, Sam. I think what Corbett wanted to avoid was a fight.'

They put platters and cups atop the old dining table, brought coffee over, and sat down to eat. It had been a long time since their last meal.

Later, they went over to the bunkhouse to fire up the iron stove. Sam thought Gus and Jim would probably not make it all the way back until close to midnight, if they drove straight on through, and he was doubtful that they would do that. They had bedrolls and grub, they could make a camp and not even try to roll in until tomorrow.

Dick crossed over to the main-house, which had been his uncle's residence. It was dingy inside, smelled of woodsmoke and greasy cooking, and had a number of forlorn mementoes of Manuel Dutra's early days in the basin. For example, there was an old Indian lance complete with coup feathers, leaning in a corner where Manuel had probably propped it twenty years earlier because he did not know what else to do with the thing. There was also a dim, darkening tintype of Manuel and two other men hanging above the black old stone fireplace. All three men were unsmiling and armed to the teeth.

Dick had thought, months back when he'd first arrived at the ranch, that someday, when he had the time, he'd knock holes in some of the walls and install windows, and bring in furniture that a person could sit on in comfort.

Tonight he was tired, so he made himself a drink of whiskey and water in the kitchen, took it to the parlour, kicked off his boots and dropped down in the only comfortable chair in the room to roll a smoke to go with his branch-watered-whiskey.

He had for a fact, indulged in a lot of guesswork. If old Brackett turned up Dick was going to look like a genuine horse's rear end, not only out on the range, but also in town. And that actually had been a fairly far-out guess he'd made about Barney Brackett.

About Singletary he had no doubts at all. He had never before heard of a rustling operation this cleverly planned, nor executed on such a big scale. After studying John Singletary he had decided Brackett's

67

rangeboss was capable of master-minding something like this. Whatever else Singletary was, he was a smart man.

Two things he would have bet his life on; those were his long yearlings up in that mountain meadow, and John Singletary had devised the most lucrative way to make a living as a cattle rustler.

He drained half the glass, smoked, considered those unsmiling, spare men in their dingy tintype photograph over the fireplace and knew what *they* would have done in his boots; they would have ridden over there, hauled Singletary or one of his men out into the yard, pushed a cocked sixgun in someone's belly and given them ten seconds to tell the truth.

It was still a very good way to handle things, and perhaps if Marshal Corbett were not involved, it would be worth considering now.

He killed the cigarette and moodily considered what remained of his drink. Singletary's men would be down out of the mountains by tomorrow, most probably; it would not require more time to finish that marking, up in the meadow. They probably had finished with it today, in which case they probably would strike out for their home-place right after breakfast tomorrow—and *that* would make a difference. Singletary by himself was one thing, Singletary with his entire riding crew backing him up, would be another thing.

He finished the drink and was considering heading for bed when a strong fist rattled the front door. He arose wondering who would be out there this late at night, and went over to see. Sam Picket was standing there, hatless, as though perhaps Sam had also been about to retire. He raised an arm to point westward, and said, 'I was makin' my last round of the barn, and heard the wagon coming . . . Listen.'

Dick stepped outside. It was an utterly still, starbright night with the cold increasing. He could very distinctly hear the wagon. He had heard a lot of wagons in his time, but that old war-wagon had a heavier, more solid grumble than other wagons. He cocked an eye at Sam. 'I didn't expect them until tomorrow. Gus must have got impatient.'

Sam shrugged and dropped his arm. Down at the barn a lantern sputtered to life and Frank Longtree's shadow appeared in the doorway as he carried the lantern toward the tie-rack.

Sam and Dick walked down there. Frank nodded to Dick and draped the old lantern from a peg on the front of the barn, then cocked his head.

The wagon was not hastening, but it was steadily grinding over gritty soil. Even so, the three waiting men had to be content with killing a full quarter of an hour before that big, squatty, ugly old wagon came into sight around the north side of the barn and ground ponderously toward the light.

Jim and Gus were bundled into their coats. They looked rumpled and lumpy in the poor light as Gus stopped the hitch, set the binders, slackened the lines and stolidly gazed at the three men over by the tie-rack. Then Gus jerked a meaty thumb. 'Go look in the back,' he said, leaning to climb down. Jim Jones, younger and more agile, came down over the side to the hub, and from there to the ground in one long, fluid glide. He walked back, ignored Sam, Frank and Dick to begin unlooping the chain, and by the time he was ready to lower the oaken tailgate, Gus was back there to lend a hand. Not a word was spoken until the tailgate was down, then Gus said, 'Jim, fetch that light, will you?'

While Jones was gone Gus grunted his way up inside the wagon where their bedrolls and grub boxes were, shoved things aside; and when Jim returned, holding the light aloft so that it shone adequately inside the wagon, Gus leaned and hauled back a soiled and stained old canvas. The light fell on a grey, dead face.

Frank, Dick and Sam were like stone with shock.

Gus dropped the canvas to one side and turned a bitter face to say, 'Brackett.'

For moments there was not a sound. Gus leaned again, grabbed the dead man's ankles and began roughly sliding the corpse toward the open end of the wagon where it could be grasped and lifted out. He grunted his way back down to the ground and said, 'Lend a hand. We'd best take him into the barn and cover him. Jim, fetch that old canvas.'

They carried Barney Brackett into the barn with Jim coming along, still carrying the lantern, and now also burdened with that old canvas.

They were placing the dead man in a stall when Dick said, 'Where did you find him, Gus?'

'Down a ravine where he'd been covered with some rocks—but not covered very well. The coyotes were having a hey-day digging him out. We heard their yapping and went over there. It wasn't quite dark.' Gus shoved back his hat, and pulled off his gloves while gazing at the lined, weathered face of the corpse, then roughly leaned and pushed dirt off, lifted half of the dead man's coat, and pointed. 'Bullet hole. He got shot from in back, but I'd say the other feller wasn't very far away—maybe beside him or just a little ahind him. The hole don't look so bad in front, but if you roll him over . . . It was a sixgun—or a damned cannon. He's got a hell of a hole in his back.' Gus straightened around looking into the shadowy faces. 'Want to hear how I figure this, Dick?'

Sam Picket answered. 'Singletary. Him and his crew are raidin' hell out of old Brackett's ranch.'

71

Gus considered Picket for a long moment, then sounded a little disappointed when he said, 'Yeah; but how did you guess it?'

Dick gestured. 'Toss the canvas over him, Gus. Let's go over to the bunkhouse and have a drink.'

The last man out of the barn was Jim Jones, still carrying the old lantern. He blew it out on the bunkhouse porch and left it hanging out there on a wooden peg.

Frank did not come inside, he went out to care for the team-horses, and by he time he got in where it was light and heat, Gus and Dick had pretty well talked themselves out.

Gus was hanging his old coat and hat from the nail above his bunk when he said, 'You should have kept Dan Corbett here.'

The answer to that, of course, was that Dick had not had enough evidence to compel the lawman to return to the home-place with them, and certainly, none of them had had any idea what Gus and Jim would return home with.

Sam Picket shoved a scantling into the stove. It was already warm enough in the log bunkhouse, but Sam wanted fire under the big coffeepot atop the stove. He also dug out a bottle of whiskey and set it upon the big old bunkhouse table. He was going after tin cups when he said, 'Any sign of Brackett's riding crew in the foothills, Gus? They should have finished up on those cattle by noon.'

72

There had been no sign of riders, nor of anything else for that matter, until Gus and Jim had been attracted by the ruckus over in that draw where the coyotes had been digging. 'Empty country,' he told Sam. 'Not even no cattle or horses . . . We decided to haul all the way back tonight, in case Dick wants someone to go to town for the law . . .' Gus sat down at the old table and, lamp-glow from in front cast his bear-like shadow on the back wall; it looked twice as large, and more bear-like than ever.

'Jim and I figure that someone'll most likely go back up that draw maybe tomorrow, and when they find Brackett gone and our wagon tracks . . .'

Frank said, 'Why tomorrow? No reason to go look at a grave, Gus.'

Gus Hanson ran bent fingers through his thick beard as he watched Sam put some cups on the table. As he reached for one he said, 'Yes there is, Frank. Whoever pitched old Brackett down there was in a hurry; he didn't pile enough rocks over the body. Sure as hell he'll do something about that as soon as he can.

Dick crossed to a door-side bunk and sat down upon the edge of it. Sam handed him one of the tin cups which contained coffee and whiskey. He nodded his thanks then wagged his head. He had not known Barney Brackett, and from what he had observed and heard, felt no particular sense of loss. But even the Devil deserved better than to be shot in the back, dumped down a draw and then have rocks dumped atop him.

This affected him for what it was—a bushwhacking murder—but what he had been thinking while his riders were gloomily talking had little to do with Barney Brackett. After Gus finished offering his opinion why the killer would go back up there, Dick said, 'He'd be smart not to wait until tomorrow, Gus. It'd be better to finish burying the corpse in the dark . . . tonight.'

They thought about that while sipping the laced coffee. It had not just a warming effect, but also a livening one. Even unsmiling Gus Hanson loosened a little. He leaned on the old table staring at the door. 'It's a long ride,' he said, without sounding reluctant to make it, 'and if you're right, Dick . . .' He swilled some laced coffee, then finished by saying, 'The son of a bitch will maybe already have been there when we get back up there. Or—maybe he'll still be up there.' Gus turned a malevolent gaze upon his employer. 'Maybe, by golly, he will be at that.' He drained the cup and set it aside. 'Let's get saddled up.' He was almost smiling. 'We can give that son of a bitch something to think about . . . hang him on the spot, then dump him in that ravine and pitch rocks down on him.'

Dick's answer was brief. 'You and Jim stay

on the ranch, Gus. Sam, Frank and I'll ride up there.'

Hanson's brows dropped stormily. 'What the hell for?' he demanded.

'Because when Marshal Corbett finds out in town that Brackett didn't take the stage out of Butterfield for Denver, he's goin' to come out there. He said he'd do that, and someone's got to be here when he rides in.'

Hanson would not yield. 'You don't know which draw it is, Dick. In the dark you'd maybe ride right past it. You don't need two men here when Dan Corbett arrives . . . Jim can stay here to fetch the marshal on up here, and I'll ride back and show you which draw it was.'

Chase stood up and flapped his arms in resignation. Sam Picket turned toward the stove to conceal a crooked little smile. As he had said this afternoon, Gus Hanson was a very pig-headed man.

CHAPTER EIGHT

KING

Jim Jones watched them depart with mixed feelings. He did not like the idea of being left behind, but it was becoming increasingly cold and the warm bunkhouse had definite appeal to him.

He knew what he was to do; wait in the yard until Marshal Corbett arrived tomorrow, then take him up where the grave was. As he went inside the bunkhouse for more of that laced coffee he decided it was not so bad being left behind.

The cold *was* increasing, although it was a long way from midnight when Dick led his riders back toward the distant foothills. But the men had their coats. What they really lacked was sufficient rest. This had been an extraordinarily long day.

Gus Hanson, as usual, looked like a grizzly bear on his horse, and he was about as talkative as one too, until they were crossing Brackett range and heard horses up ahead somewhere, in the darkness, then Gus methodically unbuttoned his coat to have easier arm movement in the area of his sixgun holster and pointed northeasterly. 'Sounds like about the right number—four or five of them.'

Shrewd Sam Pickett resolved the tension with a knowledgeable remark. 'Loose-stock,' he said. 'They're unshod and there's no sound of leather. Most likely ours since there's no stock of Brackett's over here.'

They were unable to determine whether those loose horses belonged to Dick Chase or not because as soon as the distant animals heard mounted men approaching, they fled southward like the wind.

Frank chuckled. 'If Jim had been along he'd

76

have rushed out there.'

They did not have the up-ended foothill country in sight until they were close enough to feel the warmer air. If there had been at least a half-moon it might have helped. Dick, however, was not thinking of how things *should* be, he was thinking of how they *were*, so he halted his men at the face of the first rocky upthrusts and motioned.

'Frank, go out and around . . . Gus, just where is that ravine?'

Hanson pointed again. 'East of us and ahead maybe a mile.'

'Frank, go around from the left,' Dick reiterated. 'Gus, ride eastward, and be damned careful.'

Frank was scratching his head. 'How am I goin' to know where you fellers'll be?'

Sam drily said, 'You'll hear us.'

When Gus and Frank had departed Sam stepped off his horse to thumb the *cincha*, and to expectorate, then he gazed at his employer across the saddle-seat. 'Keep an eye on Gus,' he said quietly.

They then rode directly northward past brakes and flaky stonepiles where underbrush struggled to survive. They passed small stands of trees, mostly stunted pines, and halted from time to time to listen and look.

Gus was nowhere in sight. They could no longer even hear Frank Longtree. Sam jettisoned his cud and leaned on the

77

saddlehorn to say, 'A man makes a big target when he's settin' atop a horse.'

They rode a few more yards, then dismounted and led the animals. A big owl sitting on the ground turned to stare at them. There was a varmint hole nearby. If the owl was waiting for something to crawl out of that hole, he was likely to have an hour's long wait.

The owl fluffed its feathers as the men walked past leading horses, but did not offer to fly nor hop away.

In the distance they abruptly heard a large rock rattle among other rocks. Dick looked at Sam then continued to walk, but he corrected their course now so as to be heading in the direction of that sound.

It did not necessarily have to be someone up there pitching rocks away looking for Brackett's corpse; in this kind of unstable country every change in weather sent large and small stones tumbling from the piles of rocks to the lower areas.

They found a ravine with underbrush growing down in it. There were a few widely separated pine trees along here too, but underbrush predominated. During the working season there was water down there, but this late in the year there was nothing but doughy dark mud. Still, the underground water-table was probably high otherwise even hardy underbrush would not still be flourishing.

Dick stepped close to a large old pine tree. His horse's head was up, little ears pointing directly ahead. The animal had either heard or scented something; most probably the latter because neither Sam nor Dick had detected any sound after hearing the boulder rattle loose.

For a while neither Sam nor Dick moved, then Dick handed Picket his reins and gave his head a little negative shake, in this fashion conveying his meaning for Picket to remain with the horses.

They were both satisfied this was the correct ravine, but how far up it Dick might have to walk before finding anything was a different matter. Gus had said about a mile—which could easily be closer to two miles—but to a man on foot who was not accustomed to going anywhere very far on foot, even a half-mile seemed interminably long, and by the time Dick had covered a couple of hundred yards the underbrush up ahead began to thin out, as though perhaps the water-table up in here was not as close to the surface as it had been back where he had left Sam and the horses.

There were a few more pine trees along the upper slopes of the ravine on both sides, except for this Dick would have been pretty well in the open.

He stopped beside one particular tree; it had been bent half over as a sapling, probably by the weight of winter snows, and although it was now a very large pine, perhaps about seventy-five years old, it still had that warped, uneven look to it.

There was not a sound for a long while, then from the east Dick heard the faint echo of shod hooves crossing shale-rock soil, and moments later he also heard something else directly ahead up the creek, and this time he could make a closer assessment of the sound because he had heard it nearly every day of his life; a man was pushing a saddlehorse up a slope of crumbly earth, and cursing at the animal when it faltered or grunted to lunge ahead.

He made a guess; that man up ahead had also heard the shod-horse sounds coming in from the east, which was the direction from which Gus Hanson would be approaching; and without knowing it was Gus, the man riding up out of the ravine knew all he had to know, which was simply that he was not alone up here where there was no reason for anyone else to be.

What he probably had not had time to guess was that there were two other men up here too. Dick eased back a little when the lunging horse reached the top-out. The horse and rider were faintly silhouetted up there. The man was holding his rein-hand high, as though prepared to turn in any direction, and he was sitting twisted in the saddle looking back where those shod-horse sounds were growing gradually more distinct.

Dick rugged the tie-down loose over his holstered Colt, slowly lifted the gun to belly-level and held it aimed. The man ahead had three directions to ride in. Dick thought he would turn southward, but until the rider actually did this, there was no certainty that he would.

The rangerider walked his horse along the rim of the ravine where the earth was not as gritty as elsewhere, and made almost no noise at all. But he was a perfect target up there, if Gus came along, saw him and decided to try a shot.

But Gus did not appear. The sounds of a rider coming from his direction abruptly ceased. Dick had no time to speculate about that because the rangerider was now less than a hundred yards in front of him. He eased around the disfigured pine tree, came out upon the far side and leaned. The rider was now more confident, evidently, because he was no longer concentrating on what was behind him and upon the far side of the ravine, he was looking forward as well.

Dick was certain of one thing. As wary as that horseman was acting, when he was challenged he very well might go for his gun.

The distance lessened, Dick re-gripped his Colt, listened to the faint-soft sound of the oncoming horse, pulled back until he could see up there with one side of his face, then he cocked the sixgun and when the rangeman was less than forty feet distant, Dick moved partially into view and called softly.

'Hold it right where you are!'

The horse was equally as astonished as was the man, and without awaiting rein-pressure the horse stopped dead still, ears rigidly pointing.

The rider saw half a human silhouette behind a crooked tree. Dick understood the value of surprise. He did not allow the rider to get set. 'Get down on the off-side of your horse, and keep both hands in plain sight. *Get down!*'

The man leaned as though to kick free and swing off, then perhaps the moment of shock had passed, because he hesitated, peering intently toward Dick and the crooked tree. Dick stepped into plain view and tilted the barrel of his cocked sixgun. 'Off,' he snarled. 'Give me even a little excuse and I'll kill you.' That was plain enough. The rangeman came down on the off-side of his horse, both hands clear of his sides. He turned and looked steadily at Dick Chase, who walked a little closer so that his captive could see that his sixgun was cocked. The man did not look familiar, but Dick had not expected him to, he did not know Brackett's riders. He said, 'Shuck that gunbelt. Don't touch the gun. Let the whole belt fall.'

Again the rangerider seemed to hesitate.

Dick did not move. The rangeman reluctantly unbuckled the belt and let it fall. Then he spoke, finally, 'Who the hell do you think you are? This here is Brackett range and Mister Brackett don't take kindly to trespassers.'

Evidently the rangeman did not know who Dick was either. He enlightened him. 'My name is Chase. I'm on the Dutra place. That establishes who *I* am. Now who the hell are *you*?'

The cowboy stared hard at Dick. There must have been a number of disconnected thoughts racing through his mind. He may not have answered, he did not seem to be willing to, when a big barrel-shaped ominous dark shadow appeared without a sound not more than fifty feet behind the man. Dick recognised Gus at once, wondered where his horse was and how he had managed to cross the ravine and get down here without a sound; then Gus swore in his menacing tone of voice and started ahead, both mighty arms extended, bear-like. The rangeman gave a little start and half twisted. He saw enough to frighten him, and instead of facing forward where the deadly gun was, he instinctively spun and crouched to face the more visually terrifying aspect of a man who looked like a bear coming for him.

He probably should have taken to his heels and run westerly, except that he could not have gone very far. The fastest man on earth could not outdistance a bullet. And on foot he would not have done very well in another way; Frank Longtree was riding toward the sounds of those voices, from the west.

Gus Hanson growled deep down, then laughed. He was completely contemptuous of the man raising gnarled fists and waiting. Well, Gus could be. He was no taller than the rangerider but he was easily seventy pounds heavier.

Dick eased down the hammer of his Colt and considered calling to Gus to leave it be. Instinct told him he might just as well order the pine tree at his back to stop growing.

Gus was surprisingly light on his feet, something the men he had worked with down the years had never stopped marvelling at. He came shuffling ahead, paused then went slightly sideways, like a crab, and the cowboy shifted stance to face in this new direction. He had his right fist cocked high and his left hand thrust slightly ahead to paw at Hanson. Evidently he had been in his share of brawls.

Gus turned back to his right, shuffling along, and the moment the rangeman also faced half around, Gus changed leads in mid-stride and with grace and speed his opponent could not have expected, went dead ahead. The cowboy fired his cocked fist. That was the only blow he was able to throw, and it missed.

Gus caught the man around the chest, pinning one arm, and with square white teeth showing in a grimace, locked both hands in back and tightened his grip. It was exactly the tactic bears used. The cowboy tried to rain blows around Hanson's head with his free fist, but he was too close, the blows fell harmlessly.

Gus leaned back, lifted the cowboy six inches, then swung him and dropped with the cowboy under him. The man got off half a scream before the breath was crushed out of him.

Frank rode up, stopped and sat his saddle.

Gus heaved halfway up off the rangeman, placed one huge paw of a hand around the man's gullet and started to squeeze. The cowboy tried feebly to tear the fingers away, but he was too dazed to accomplish anything. Gus lifted the man half off the ground and shook him like a rat, then released him and rocked back on his heels, waiting.

Dick walked over. He felt sorry for the rangeman but only to the extent to see that Gus did not start in on him again. He said, 'What's your name?'

The battered, half-dazed man offered only a fleeting glance up at Dick Chase. He was staring in raw fear at massive, bewhiskered Gus Hanson. With a gloved hand to his gullet he rasped out a quick answer.

'Wesley King.'

Dick motioned. 'Get up.'

King made an effort. Gus leaned, caught him by the shirt and arose bringing Wesley King up with him. Gus released the man and looked over at Frank. They winked at each other in the ghostly light.

Dick leathered his weapon, picked up King's weapon and pitched it over the lip of the ravine down into the underbrush. 'Who do you work for?' he asked, and got back another instantaneous answer.

'For Mister Brackett.'

Dick considered the man. He was about average in height and build, and had an unshorn head of dark hair where his hat had been. He was probably close to thirty years of age. In most ways he was nondescript. Dick said, 'Where is Mister Brackett?'

Wesley King glanced past at Frank Longtree, sitting up there bleak in the face and unfriendly. He did not look around at Gus again. 'He went to Denver to see an eye doctor.'

Gus casually said, 'You lyin' bastard.'

Wesley King shot Gus a darting glance, then would not look in his direction again. Dick Chase seemed the least menacing of the three men facing him. 'That's what John Singletary told us. Mister Brackett's had failin' eyesight for a long time. He decided to go up to—'

'When did he go?' Dick asked.

Wesley King stopped gingerly massaging his throat. 'I got no idea. Me'n the other riders was up in the mountains markin' some cattle.'

Gus growled again. '*Our* cattle. Dick, let's hang the son of a bitch.'

86

Dick did not agree nor disagree; he said, 'What were you doin' back up in that ravine?'

Now, finally, they were down to the crux of things. Wesley King's eyes moved rapidly. He seemed about to speak, then he seemed about not to speak.

Gus's scorn was monumental. 'I'll break both his arms, Dick. He'll start talkin' like a little ol' granny.'

Dick said, 'Frank, fetch his horse. Let's get on home. Corbett'll be interested in what we got an' what he was doing when we caught him.'

Longtree reined over to the patient-standing horse and led it up. Gus sneered at Wesley King, then turned without another word and went slipping and sliding down the ravine to cross it to the spot where he had left his own horse.

Frank led King's animal back where Sam Picket was waiting. He too had heard the commotion up yonder and was anxious by the time Dick walked up on foot and took back the reins to his animal. Dick jerked a thumb and said, 'He works for Singletary. He'll tell us the rest of it when we get back home.'

Sam scowled. 'Where's Gus?'

'Across the creek. He'll meet us down yonder below the foothills. Get mounted, Sam.'

CHAPTER NINE

GUS SPEAKS

Gus probably would not have spoken to Wesley King on the ride back, but Dick made sure neither Sam nor Frank would either by simply setting the example. It was a long ride, it was cold, King had a sore body from his shellacking by Gus Hanson, and without being spoken to for several hours did not help King's morale.

Nor had Dick Chase expected it to be otherwise.

Dawn was close when they reached the yard, doggedly swung off, left Gus watching the prisoner while they cared for their animals, then came back to the front hitch-rack looking tired, grey and whiskery.

Jim Jones came from the direction of the cookshack, stared at the prisoner, then told the others he was rassling up some breakfast. They all trooped over where it was warm and fragrant.

Jim had hot coffee, which was a blessing, and while it was uncharacteristic of him, he worked at the stove instead of staring at the prisoner, and talking his head off.

Wesley King's condition improved when he was inside the warm cookshack and had some hot coffee inside him, but the enduring silence bothered him, so he eventually said, 'I just ride for Mister Brackett, that's all.'

Frank was scratching a leathery, whiskery cheek when he said, 'Yeah; like I ride for the devil in hell,' and ignored King to reach for his coffee cup.

Gus leaned and tapped King with a thick finger. 'What were you doin' up yonder in the ravine?' Gus offered no admonition to King about telling the truth, he simply continued to lean across the table looking icily into the rangeman's eyes.

King looked into his two-thirds empty cup before answering. During the silence Sam Picket offered King some advice. 'Cowboy, you're goin' to get your head beat soft if you don't speak up and get it over with . . . We know most of it anyway.'

King raised his eyes, considered Sam, and probably decided Picket was the least hostile, so he kept looking at Sam when he finally replied.

'We come back to the ranch late this afternoon . . . Finished with them heifers in plenty of time to . . .'

'What were you doin' up that damned ravine?' Gus snarled, leaning harder, and with both powerful arms atop the table.

'John sent me up there after we'd all got back to the ranch.'

'What for, did he send you up there?'

89

' . . . He said . . . '

Gus started to rise up across the table, and no one appeared willing to stop him. The cowboy swallowed hastily and started over.

'John told me to go back up the ravine where there was a dead man and pile rocks on him.' Having said that, Wesley King seemed to have got the worst of it out.

Dick had a question. 'Who was the dead man?'

'Someone John said who was tryin' to steal cattle . . . I found where someone had flung rocks down, but hell, if there'd been a man under there, he'd rose up and gone away because that grave was empty.'

Gus remained on his feet. He did a surprising thing, for him, he took his cup and Wesley King's cup over where Jim was standing by the stove, watching, re-filled them both and returned to the table where he put King's cup in front of the rangeman without a word.

Dick said, 'Gus, take him over to the barn. Frank, go with them. Then fetch him back here.'

King arose looking worried. When Gus shoved him toward the door King looked back as though to plead, but he said nothing, and neither did anyone else.

After Singletary's rider had departed with Longtree and Hanson, Dick glanced at Sam Picket. 'He could be tellin' the truth.'

Sam's mouth drooped. 'Naw. Well; maybe that part of it was the truth, Dick, but as sure as I'm settin' here him and the other riders been stealin' cattle all along, and they knew those weren't Brackett's heifers when they marked them.'

Dick emptied his coffee cup and shoved it away. He believed that what Picket had said about the rangeriders working for Singletary was true. From the beginning he had thought Singletary and his riders were rustlers. But he was not convinced right now that the other cattle thieves knew that Singletary had killed Barney Brackett. *He* was convinced of it, but there was no proof. What he had hoped was that Wesley King would have known who was under those rocks in the ravine. That would have been all the proof he—and more importantly, Marshal Corbett—would need.

Gus and Frank came stamping back across the cook-shack porch with their badly shaken companion. When they shoved King back into the warmth and light, Dick and Sam were waiting. They saw the look on King's face—he *hadn't* known.

Frank eased back down at the old table and gazed wryly at his employer. He did not say a word, but Gus Hanson did, as he also sat back down and reached for his half-full cup. 'This son of a bitch is a natural-born darned liar.'

King spoke in quick protest. 'So help me, Mister Chase, I didn't know it would be Mister

91

Brackett under them stones. I never even had an inkling it was him.'

Dick began working up a cigarette and did not speak until he was finished and had lighted up. Then, trickling smoke and gazing in an almost detached manner at Wesley King, he said, 'How long have you fellers been rustling cattle off Brackett?'

King was grey in the face. The shock of seeing Barney Brackett dead under that dirty old canvas had shaken him badly. Even so, he hung fire over answering Chase's direct question. He reached with a shaking hand for his cup of coffee. Wordlessly, Gus caught him by the wrist, took away the cup, shoved it out of reach and released the wrist.

Dick said it again. 'How long?'

' . . . Jesus; listen, Mister Chase, I never was really—'

'How long!'

'. . . Since John got himself hired on as Mister Brackett's foreman. We was camped in the mountains . . . He got rid of the other riders and pretended to hire us on one at a time . . . Since then, Mister Chase.'

'How many have you stolen?'

'I don't rightly know. About half, or more, I'd guess.

'How did you get rid of them?'

'John and Ernie Black would trail 'em out two, three hundred head at a time while the rest of us fellers worked the range . . . There

92

was a feller named Scaggs waitin' to take 'em over. He had his two sons with him. Scaggs would pay John and take the cattle south where he could ship 'em to Kansas City.'

'Without a bill of sale signed by Brackett?'

' . . . Well no; John give Scaggs a bill of sale.'

Sam Picket let go a big rattling sigh and went over to refill his coffee cup. As he turned back he looked steadily at Wesley King. Sam had helped hang rustlers for doing far less than Singletary and his gang had done.

Dick said, 'About my long yearlings . . .'

King did not hesitate now. 'John and Ernie seen 'em . . . We went after 'em one night when they was grazin' over near the boundary line. We took 'em up to that big meadow where we worked 'em, finishin' up today.'

Jim Jones was trying to alternately listen and cook. He was doing better at the former than at the latter, until Frank Longtree suddenly arose when he smelled burning meat, went over and swore at the curled, black meat in the iron skillets, and shoved Jim away to finish the cooking.

Jim took coffee over to the table and re-filled all the cups, then returned the pot to the stove and stood over there gazing at Wesley King, who was not much older than Jim was.

Outside, daylight was on its way, the sun was visible and nightlong shadows were dissipating, but it was still cold out there.

Dick said, 'They're goin' to wonder why you

93

haven't come back,' to Wesley King, and got a nod from the rustler about that. Dick looked around. 'Frank, is the grub ready?'

Longtree shot Jim a malevolent glance as he replied. 'Yeah, it was ready a half-hour ago but—well—anythin' is better'n a snowbank, isn't it? Jim, fetch those plates!'

They ate without speaking, and because they were hungry men there was not a single comment upon the condition of their fried meat and spuds, but almost any other time there would have been.

Wesley King did not eat. Jim put a plate before him but he ignored it to roll and light a smoke. His hands were no longer shaking, but his colour had not as yet returned to normal. Looking at a dead man inside a gloomy old log barn when he had not expected anything like that, had destroyed more than his appetite, it also demoralised him.

Sam Picket was looking at his employer when he said, 'When will Dan get out here?'

Dick had no idea, and he was not really thinking about the marshal. 'Whenever he does, it'll likely be too late, Sam. Singletary is no fool. When King don't return, he'll guess about what happened—someone else was up there where he buried Brackett.' Dick put down his knife and fork and glanced at the drawn, whiskery faces of his rangemen. 'My guess is that they've just about cleaned out Brackett. Otherwise why would they steal our heifers? That bein' so, if Singletary gets spooked, they'll quit the country in a hurry.'

Wesley King volunteered a statement. 'John said when he sent us up to mark them heifers, they'd be the last bunch we'd trail over to Mister Scaggs.'

Dick nodded about that and shoved away his plate and cup. 'We've been a hell of a long time without sleep.'

Frank Longtree held his cup in mid-air when he replied to that. 'Sure, and if we bed down now, and Singletary is spooked, we'll sleep right through it when him and his bastards leave the country.'

Dick did not respond. That was exactly what he knew, but it bothered him to push his men still more. Every one of them except Jim Jones had been in the saddle since yesterday morning, early. They had just finished their first hot meal since then; they looked grey and haggard. He himself was tired to the bone, so the others had to be that way too.

Gus Hanson, who was still shovelling in food and appearing not to listen, continued to shovel it in as he growled around the mouthfuls. 'We can get some sleep, and still make it over there.'

No one asked how this could be accomplished, they sat looking at Gus and waiting. After a moment of furious chewing, then swallowing, Gus said, 'We got a war-wagon, don't we? Jim can drive it, he's rested up. The rest of us can lie in the back on blankets and sleep until we're over there . . . It'll be a little bouncy and all, but who the hell ever said everything in this lousy life was meant to be comfortable and tidy?'

CHAPTER TEN

A BEAUTIFUL MORNING

Gus Hanson's suggestion seemed to be the answer, a bizarre one which required a little querying and mumbling—and finally laughing—as they hauled bedrolls over, guns, ammunition, and even some food, while Jim went after the big team which had pulled the wagon before.

They left the yard in the cold of early morning and, as Gus had thought, only very exhausted men could have slept behind the oak sideboards, but they slept—awakened when Jim was not sufficiently diligent in avoiding particularly bad buffalo wallows and chuck-holes, swore soundly—then slept some more.

They looked completely disreputable, but their stomachs were full, they were getting rest, of a sort, and their resolve had not wavered even before Gus had come up with his unique idea.

But Frank Longtree had not thought it was such a strange idea; he had told them days ago what that massively cumbersome and impregnable wagon had originally been built for, which was exactly what they were now using it for, although they did not believe they would actually need a War-wagon when they got to the Brackett place. But that also was something they could have speculated about, except that they did not, they simply dropped amid blankets, weapons, and grub boxes, and slept.

Jim Jones may not have been the best teamster on the Dutra place when he started out, but after some thunderous and blistering imprecations came up out of the boxed-in wagonbed, he became at least as adept as anyone else at watching for the worst bumps.

He was their eyes, but for a couple of hours they did not need that, and when he eventually saw what appeared to be several horsemen far ahead, southwesterly in the direction of the Brackett home-place, he considered waking the men behind and below him. Ordinarily he would have shouted first and made certain second. This time he elected to be more circumspect; those furious tongue-lashings had had good effect.

It was not horsemen, it was a small bunch of wet cows with wobbly-legged new calves which had separated from a herd somewhere to calve in privacy, and afterwards to make their own

97

little group.

The cold lessened, sunshine did not reach down inside the wagon but the heat increased enough to make conditions a little less trying for Sam, Dick, Frank and Gus. By the time Gus struggled into a sitting position to grope for a canteen, the war-wagon was two-thirds of the way across Dutra range. The invisible boundary line was in Jim's sight, recognisable in a general way by the trees—called witness trees—which marked the approximate survey line between the two cow outfits.

Gus heaved up to his feet, leaned on the two-inch-thick scored, scarred, and thoroughly dry, iron-like oaken sideboard nearest him, and spat as he squinted ahead. He knew about where they were. Jim Jones also did, but Gus growled at him to haul a little more to the south, and Jim obeyed. The man lying, with his ankles and wrists bound, directly below the driver's high seat was the most vivid visual evidence of what occurred when other men contradicted or challenged Gus, or did neither of those things but still earned his dislike.

Gus stepped around the jiggling bodies and got to the rear of the high seat. 'Can you see the buildings from here?' he asked.

Jim couldn't. All he could see was hundreds of miles of open cow-country. 'Not yet. Be another half-hour or so.

Gus accepted that and, holding to the front of the wagon-box, turned to scan the southeastern plain as well as the northeastern plain. He had half-expected to see Marshal Corbett back there whipping right along with a big posse of townsmen. All he saw was a little band of wet cows with baby calves standing perfectly still out a short distance, staring at the massive, lumbering wagon.

Gus evidently had had all the sleep he thought he needed. Instead of dropping down again he systematically began examining all the Winchesters they had brought along. He did not find a single one of them which was not fully loaded, with a cartridge in the chamber under the hammer. Gus sat there holding the last carbine, staring at the tailgate. His father had been a hard-shell Baptist Bible-banger. No one knew this because Gus never talked about his personal experiences or antecedents. His father, also bull-built and perfectly willing to wrestle the devil or back-sliders, had thundered to Gus as a child about the absolute evil of guns.

Gus sighed and considered the grey, scarred old saddlegun in his lap. His father had been right, there was probably nothing under the sun as evil as a gun—and in another way, nothing as reassuring to handle, or as perfectly adapted to keep a man alive in hostile country, or as necessary as long as other men used guns.

He put the weapon aside and felt around for his tobacco, and that was something else his father had been unbendingly vociferous about. Next to whiskey and guns, in that order, tobacco was the devil's weed; it stunted a man's growth, sapped his virility, clogged up his lungs, ruined his appetite, sneakily and surely destroyed his memory and eventually his eyesight.

Gus lit up and trickled smoke past his bearded lips, and smiled, which was something he did not do often, nor without reason.

Jim spoke, jarring Gus out of his reverie. 'I can see the buildings.'

Gus leaned and slapped Sam lightly on the shoulder. Sam sat up, cleared his pipes and expertly expectorated completely over the high sides of the wagon, then he awakened Dick and Frank Longtree.

The morning was well along, sunlight reached down into the wagon-bed over the waist-high sides, the team was sweating and Jim Jones had moved his Winchester from beside him to between his knees. He had his hat tipped down and from beneath the brim was intently studying the clutch of old log buildings on ahead in the middle distance.

The other men also looked in that direction from over the sides of the wagon. Not a word was said for a long time, then Jim spoke again, 'It's awful quiet down there. Maybe they already left.'

No one commented. The prisoner on the floor of the wagon was watching the armed men, he could not see much else from inside the wagon-box. Dick spat, looked around at Wesley King, watched the prisoner for a moment then turned back to do as the others were also doing, but when they were clearly in view of the yard he said, 'Duck down. If there's no one there—well then we've had a long ride for nothing, but if there is someone there . . .'

They all sank back down behind the sideboards.

The war-wagon and its powerful big team-horses were the only moving things for miles. If someone was at the Brackett home-place by now they would have noticed the wagon. But when no one appeared Jim reiterated what he had observed before.

'Hell; it's abandoned sure as I'm settin' up here.'

Frank drily said, 'You better hope it is. You make a better target than a bird on a rock.'

It took time to reach the buildings. No wagon moved swiftly unless its team was whipped up, and a vehicle as heavy as the old war-wagon did not move swiftly even then, nor was it designed to.

Frank Longtree finished in a shirt pocket, brought forth a fresh plug of chewing tobacco, and sliced off a corner which he worked up into his cheek. He removed his hat and eased up just enough to be able to see over the side-boards. To the others he said, 'Just about in Winchester range . . . Hey, hell, there's someone down there. I just saw a man come out of the bunkhouse and stand a moment lookin' out here, then he walked down to the barn.'

Gus grumbled a question. 'Carryin' anything?'

'No.'

'Then I expect they aren't ready to pull out yet . . . You see anything else?'

For a while Frank was silent. Jim Jones raised his left hand. 'There, on the bunkhouse porch, Frank.'

Jim had seen another man emerge from the log structure. Frank also saw him. At about this time another man ambled forth, perhaps in response to the call of the man on the porch. That pair Frank studied, then bleakly smiled about. 'They're tryin' to figure out what kind of a wagon this is.'

Dick put his hat aside also, and raised up very slowly until little more than his forehead and eyes were above the side-board. 'Three,' he murmured. 'Countin' Mister King that'd be four. Somewhere, Singletary's down there.'

Jim was beginning to feel uncomfortable under the stare of the curious men on the bunkhouse porch, or maybe it was not just the way they were staring, maybe it was also the fact that he had seen three of the rustlers, and as Frank had said, he was sitting up here as exposed as a bird on a rock. He looked around.

Dick said, 'Relax and drive right on into the yard. They see one feller driving a wagon. When we get in the yard they'll come out and we'll throw down on them.'

Frank saw Jim's expression and smiled as he picked up his carbine, automatically examined it as Gus had done, then raised eyes which had a wry twinkle to Jim Jones. 'Just flip over backwards if there's trouble,' he advised.

For the first time Wesley King spoke up. 'For Chris'sake don't drive right into the yard. They'll blow this wagon apart, and I'm in here too, remember.'

Gus turned a cold gaze upon King. 'Good,' he said, 'they'll save us from havin' to hang you.' Then Gus re-set his old hat and also reached for his saddlegun.

Dick eased back down and nudged Frank. Longtree also sat down with his back to the oak side-board. Sam Picket was smoking. He seemed as calm as a man could be, and he probably was; Sam was one of those people who, perhaps as the result of inherent fatalism, accepted his destiny the same at a supper table as in this kind of situation.

He squashed out the cigarette and called up to Jim Jones. 'How much farther?'

Jim did not reply immediately because he had seen that man emerge from the barn leading a saddled horse. But the man did not mount, he stood out by the hitch-rack also staring. 'Maybe half a mile,' Jim said, watching

103

that horseman, who, obviously, had initially from a considerable distance, seen a wagon, of which there were dozens in the area, but now, up closer, he was staring exactly as the two men on the bunkhouse porch were doing, because very clearly, this was not an ordinary wagon. It was about the same height from the ground, but both sets of wheels were at least five inches wide with thick steel tyres, and even if that pair of big sixteen-hundred-pound draft animals had not been pulling it, the wagon would have aroused curiosity because of its massively square and squatty build.

Finally, a man from the bunkhouse turned and called in the direction of Brackett's mainhouse. Moments later a man appeared over there on the veranda. He was hatless but otherwise he was fully attired and had a sagging gunbelt around his middle.

Dick eased up for a moment to gauge the distance, saw the man on the porch and eased back down as he said, 'Singletary's on the porch of Brackett's house.'

This last half-mile was like standing before a wall waiting for the firing squad to load their guns. The older men were stoic, but Jim Jones, with excellent reason, was not at all fatalistic. He said, 'Dick, don't call 'em until I've set the binders, tied the lines and have clumb down in there . . . They can blow me off this damned seat as easy as shootin' fish in a rainbarrel.'

Gus and Sam exchanged an amused look.

Dick did not answer because he could only, at best, make a guess about what was going to happen shortly now. Of one thing he was certain, his men were fired up to kill, and Singletary was not the variety of individual who would simply give up. Neither were his riders. Next to gunmen, professional killers of any kind, cattle and horse thieves were considered the best candidates for a hang-rope in the stock country. In *any* stock country.

Singletary was a successful outlaw, which meant that he was also good at eluding retribution. He was probably as old as Sam Picket, and an outlaw who could survive that long had to be very good, both at his trade, and staying alive in a country where men would hunt him down and kill him more enthusiastically then they would do the same things to wolves or cougars or cow-killing bears.

Jim saw the man on the porch of the main-house walk down from there in the direction of the bunkhouse. He was close enough finally to be able to make out the individual men, and evidently one of them recognised him as one of Chase's riders because he turned to Singletary and said, 'I've seen that driver over on Dutra range.

Jim eased up a booted foot to the brake-handle and steered his team to the edge of the big yard. From the side of his mouth, and without taking his eyes off the four men standing like statues between the barn and bunkhouse, staring, Jim said, 'I figure one's missing. There's supposed to be five, isn't there?'

Gus answered. 'Yeah. He's sitting down below you.'

Dick gave Jim Jones an order. 'Pull over to the hitch-rack in front of the barn. Get as close to the barn as you can.

Wesley King was pale. No one heeded him at all as they began to ease up onto their knees in a crouched position, Winchesters in hand, sixguns loose in their holsters, waiting and listening. They could not see out.

Frank stopped masticating on his cud of tobacco. Gus and Sam were looking ahead toward the oak planks below and behind Jim's high seat, and Dick re-set his hat, then picked up his carbine and waited for the challenging call he was sure would come when they got down near the middle of the big yard.

CHAPTER ELEVEN

BRACKETT'S YARD

Jones hauled up over beside the hitch-rack, no more than fifteen feet from that man holding the saddled horse. They exchanged a look. The man with the reins in his hand slowly drifted his gaze from Jim to the wagon which, up close, looked even more massively formidable than it did from a distance.

Then the rustler said, 'What the hell do you want?'

Jim methodically set the brakes, looped the lines, straightening up to answer only when he was satisfied that regardless of what happened next, the big horses would not be able to budge the war-wagon. Then, as he was about to speak, Dick Chase stood up with his cocked carbine pointing directly at the man with the horse, and said, 'You'll do to start with. Let go of those reins and put your hands out front.'

The astonished rustler blinked and stared, making no move to do as he had been told, or to try and draw his holstered weapon.

As Singletary and the men over at the bunkhouse looked on in equal astonishment, Gus, Sam and Frank arose, also with Winchesters, and Jim Jones grabbed the weapon between his knees; but before he could raise it, Singletary tore out a curse and sprang toward the bunkhouse door as he was drawing. He did not get the shot off because the men standing out there with him also sprang for cover and knocked Singletary sprawling inside the dingy big log room.

Gus said, 'Jim! Get down from there!'

Jones turned, gun in hand, to throw himself backwards down into the wagon-box, when the rustler with the horse whipped around to get the horse between himself and Dick's carbine, and because he only had a couple of feet to cover, he made it. Dick could have shot through the horse. Instead he tipped down his barrel and fired into the ground between the horse's feet. The result was as it would have been with any unsuspecting animal; the horse gave a tremendous leap, jerked the reins free and came down in a panicky run.

The rustler sprinted for the side of the barn and Frank dropped him when he could have reached cover with only one more jump. The rustler cried out, then rolled and although both Frank and Dick could have shot him, they allowed him to reach cover.

The rank scent of gunsmoke hung in the sparkling clear air of this beautiful day, and as echoes went one after the other upwards and outwards, there was no more gunfire.

One reason, no doubt, was because there was no window on the north side of the bunkhouse. Another reason may have been because the men inside the bunkhouse were still in too much disarray to do much of anything except try to understand what had happened. Dick used this interval to lean on the side-board as he said, 'Stay in here. I'm goin' down through the barn and out back. Sure as hell there's a back door to that bunkhouse.'

He sailed over the side-board, clutching his saddlegun, and came down on both feet, but he stumbled and had to regain balance before covering the fifteen or twenty feet to cover.

Inside, there were several stalled horses. They were fidgeting in near panic as the result of that gunfire. Dust hung in the air, nearly motionless where slanting sunshine reached in to add a little brightness to an otherwise gloomy atmosphere.

Dick did not expect to meet a rustler in there, nor did he, but when he got near the big doorless rear barn opening someone slammed a sixgun slug into the log in front of his position. They had not seen Dick, but they *had* seen his shadow, projected outward by that sunshine at his back.

Out front, the silence was blown apart by a sudden, vicious exchange of gunfire. He wondered how the rustlers could have managed that when there was no window in the bunkhouse wall for them to fire from, and decided at least one of them must have hauled the door open to shoot in the direction of the war-wagon. But the fierce reply the rustler got from the men in the wagon must have discouraged him, because after the savage exchange, silence settled again.

Dick guessed that the man who had seen his shadow, was the wounded rustler along the south side of the barn. This was a hindrance; he was not worried about the rustler actually shooting him, but he could not move and dared not even lean to look out as long as the man was there.

As with all horse-barns, there were sliding wooden windows in the wall of each stall where a man could pitch things out while he was dunging out. In the towns some people even had glass windows in those places, but not in range country. Dick could get over on the south wall and slide a couple of those panels open, and if he did the rustler over there would hear him doing it. But what was in Dick Chase's mind was not leaning out to shoot the man so much as diverting his attention, forcing him to worry about the open panels as well as the big rear barn doorway; *dividing* his attention.

He was edging toward the south wall when a man's shout stopped him. Someone from the bunkhouse was calling out defiant profanity. Then the curses ended and the voice said: 'Chase; you crazy son of a bitch, what do you think you're doing! When Corbett hears about you attackin' us he'll lock you up an' throw the key away! Chase . . . ?'

Dick did not respond, Sam Picket did. 'We got Wesley King in the wagon with us. That ought to let you know why we're over here. As for Dan Corbett—he's on his way. All we aim to do is keep you grounded until he gets here.'

That ended the shouting.

Dick got to the stalls, waited briefly to listen, then heaved back the first panel. It made a grating sound of wood over dry wood.

He went into the next stall and did the same thing. He knew better than to peer out, although the temptation was strong. Then he hastened back to the rear barn opening, crouched and risked a quick look. No one shot at him, so evidently his strategy had worked, that wounded rustler was more worried about being back-shot from above, from the open panels, than he was about someone looking out from the rear of the barn.

And there was indeed a rear door from the log bunkhouse, but it was firmly closed. There was also an overhang down there which protected a wash-rack where a basin stood beside a bucket with a dipper-handle sticking up out of the water.

Abruptly, someone in the war-wagon opened up on the front of the bunkhouse. He fired three times, methodically, as though he were in no hurry. A second Winchester joined in, also firing at regularly spaced intervals the way target-shooters fired their weapons.

When the firing stopped as suddenly as it had begun, someone laughed. It was an unexpected, out-of-place sound. There was one more gunshot, this time the deeper-sounding roar of a sixgun, and after that Dick heard wood splinter. Then the same man laughed again. Dick guessed it would be either Frank Longtree or Sam Picket laughing, but why they would laugh he had no idea as he inched cautiously closer to the south side of the rear opening and leaned to look again.

There was no gunshot this time either. Evidently that injured man was either being bothered by his wound, or he was snugging up to the log wall as closely as he could, peering up toward those opened panels.

For a long while there was not a sound. The air smelled of burned black powder and a little of it hung above the war-wagon. The sun was still climbing, heat began to bear down, particularly upon the men in the wagon out front of the barn. But they had canteens.

Dick crouched, gun in both hands, waiting for either the wounded man to show himself, or for someone to sneak out the rear door of the bunkhouse. What happened he had not anticipated, and it might have been fatal to him if he had not caught a sight of a moving shadow along the south barn wall, and dropped flat out of pure instinct two seconds before a sixgun nearly deafened him, and the bullet tore a ten-inch splinter of wood from the stud-log where he had been leaning.

He fired back at the shadow in front of one of those open panels, then, angry, rolled up onto his feet and levered up to fire again. He did that three times as he advanced upon the panel where the rustler had inched his way up the wall to peer inside and fire. But seconds after the rustler had fired he had dropped down again, and now he was lying below the panels, waiting.

112

Dick halted five feet from the nearest open panel, felt for fresh loads, plugged them into the carbine, and stepped ahead to lean the gun aside, draw his Colt, and edge up as close as he could get to the panel. He did not look out, he shoved his gun-hand out, tipped it down, and fired four times in rapid succession. The noise was deafening.

With one slug left, he stepped away and methodically plugged fresh cartridges from his belt into the hot-barrelled Colt. From beyond the window there was not a sound. He was not satisfied that he had hit the man, but he *was* satisfied that he had put one hell of a scare into him.

Then, freshly re-loaded, cocked sixgun in his fist, he scarcely raised his voice when he said, 'Crawl around to the back and come up where I can see you—or I'm going to blow the top off your head.'

There was no response. The silence dragged on. Dick began to suspect that he might have killed the man. He went to the saddle-pole picked up a rig which had been covered flesh-side-out, carried it to the nearest panel and moved it until it partially obscured light, and the bullet which came from below tore the saddle out of his hands and nearly sent him sprawling. The rustler out there was a long way from being dead.

Dick tried one more time; he said, 'if that flesh-out rig belonged to you—you just busted the swells all to hell.'

This time the rustler answered with spirit and venom. 'You son of a bitch, poke your head out and I'll do the same to you!'

Dick wagged his head. The rustler had a lot of fight in him, for a wounded man, and maybe his wound was not very bad after all. He returned to the rear opening to keep his vigil, but if anyone inside the bunkhouse had tried to escape by the back door, there was no sign of it. Nor was there any sign of a man being outside, and Dick's view took in a vast, broad sweep of the rangeland southerly and westward from the bunkhouse.

Gus Hanson's unmistakably booming voice sounded loudly out front. 'Come out of there, you holed-up bunch of range rats! Come out or we're goin' to set the place on fire!'

For moments there was no reply, but when it finally came the tone of the speaker matched Gus's for defiance and scorn.

'Try it, you bastard! Shootin' the door off its hinges didn't help you any. Just try gettin' over here!'

Dick waited until that exchange ended, then went back to the horse stalls, opened each door and left it open. The terrified animals required no additional encouragement to break clear, all in a panicky rush, heading for the open country which was visible past the rear barn opening. They made as much noise as a troop of charging cavalry, and Dick finally risked leaning to peer downward.

He saw the rustler. The man was tensing forward looking in the direction of the horses, completely distracted by what he might have thought would be at least one mounted man.

Dick pushed his sixgun outward and cocked it. The sound was lost in the louder noise of the terrified horses. He said, 'You move one finger and I'll kill you!'

The rustler perceptibly started to twist, then froze. He did not look up. He did not have to.

'Throw that gun away. Throw it *far* away!'

The rustler had a bloody pants'leg, his shirt and face were sweat-soaked. His hat was ten feet behind him.

'Throw it!'

The rustler lifted his right arm and hurled the gun southward. Then he slowly twisted and raised his head. He and Dick Chase stared at one another. Dick had a vague feeling about having seen this man before. 'Get up,' Dick ordered, 'and walk around the back of the barn and inside.'

'I can't stand up,' the rustler said, touching his bloody trouser-leg.

Dick moved the gunbarrel a little, until it was pointing squarely at the man's nose. 'You got up to shoot inside at me. Now stand up!' He tightened the finger inside the trigger-guard. The man watched this slight movement the same way he would have watched a rattler raise his head before striking. He reached with both hands, clawed at the log wall and heaved himself up into a standing position. He had jaw muscles straining, his sweaty face was grey, and the pain reflected in his dark eyes was like a glaze. The bloody trouser-leg concealed a broken leg.

'Start moving,' Dick said.

The rustler obeyed. It took a long time for him to cover several feet, and when he was nearing the corner of the barn, he reeled, then slid down into a sprawl.

Dick ran to the rear opening, looked out, saw that the man was not moving, and jumped ahead, grabbed cloth and began dragging the rustler, who did not either help nor resist. He was unconscious.

If someone had stepped out the rear door of the bunkhouse in that brief interval, he could have had a clear shot at Dick Chase, but no one came forth.

Dick got the wounded man inside, pushed him over onto his back, slit the soggy trouser-leg and leaned closer. The leg bone was not the extent of the rustler's injury. The bullet which had wounded him had made a long, slanting, ragged tear in the flesh and muscles before it had reached, and broken, the bone. The rustler had lost a lot of blood.

Dick looped the man's trouser-belt around the leg, twisted it with his sixgun-barrel until the bleeding stopped, then leaned back. There were two initials in gold upon the man's belt-buckle. E. B. Aside from Singletary and Wesley King, the only other name he had heard was Ernie Black. The initials fitted. The man had a wide, lipless gash of a mouth, black hair and black eyes. He was tanned nearly copper colour by exposure, and, even unconscious, had a savage, vicious cast to his features.

But he was not only tough, he was clever; wounded or not, bleeding badly, he had pulled himself up the outside logs to try and kill Dick. He had the heart of a lion, no question about that.

Dick got a steel buggy-hame to insert into the belt to replace his gunbarrel, then tied the hame so that the belt could not loosen, and stood up to wipe blood off his hands on his own trouser-legs.

Ernie Black, if that was his name, was slack and still, his barrel-chest rising in fluttery motion. Whether he would live or not, or whether he would regain consciousness or not, depended on how much blood he had lost. Dick did not think he had lost enough to die, although he had been lying out there alongside the barn since the fight had erupted. But he thought it quite likely that the man would not regain consciousness for some time.

Perhaps he should have guessed otherwise; he already knew how tough the man was. Without more than opening his black eyes, then tiredly moving his lipless mouth, the man gazed upwards and said, 'You son of a bitch!'

Dick slowly and craggily smiled. It was quite possible to have no use whatever for an enemy, and still respect and admire something about him. All men admired courage and clearly this cattle thief had it.

'Did you tie it off?'

Dick nodded. 'Yeah. The bleeding has stopped.'

'I tried to tie it off . . . out there.'

'You should have.'

'Like hell I should have. I knew you were inside the barn . . . I wanted you dead first.'

Dick slowly wagged his head. Then he said, 'Is there a bottle of whiskey cached in here?'

The black eyes did not waver, but the lids above them seemed to be getting heavy. The wounded rustler did not answer, nor make another effort to speak for a long while, then he eventually said, 'One more damned day . . .'

Dick studied the hard, clear features, then turned as someone out front yelled.

'Riders coming!'

Dick retrieved his carbine then walked toward the front barn opening. In his absence, someone had lowered the massively heavy tailgate, had let it all the way down to the ground, and had been lying behind it sniping at the bunkhouse. He was not still lying there, but Sam Picket was leaning upon the opposite side of the tailgate peering westward, his clothing dusty and dishevelled. Dick called to him quietly. 'Any of 'em get out, Sam?'

118

Picket turned, shaking his head. 'No. Frank and I shot the door off its hinges. They can't even sidle up to shoot out without Gus and Jim seein' them.' Sam gestured. 'Riders, Dick.'

It looked to be about five men, but because they were riding at a lope and all in a bunch, it was impossible to be sure.

Sam straightened up, let go a long sigh, and leaned his carbine against the lowered tailgate. 'If that's not Dan Corbett, then who the hell would it be?'

Dick did not answer because he did not know who else it might be, and also because he felt confident that it *was* Marshal Corbett.

Now, the silence was deeper than ever. For the men inside the bullet-battered old log bunkhouse, and for whom there had never really been much of a chance, there was none at all unless they chose to commit suicide by rushing forth in some wild attempt to shoot themselves clear.

They could not have covered a hundred feet. The old war-wagon was north of the broken door, with willing and ready armed men crouching at the sideboards, waiting.

Dick lifted his eyes. He had to look twice to believe it; the sun was going down over some ragged rimrocks hundreds of miles to the west.

The fight which had seemed to take no more than an hour, an hour and a half at most, had taken the entire afternoon!

CHAPTER TWELVE

DAN CORBETT

Marshal Corbett rode into the yard at a slogging walk, unsmiling, angry-eyed, and fully armed. He had three riders with him. Dick knew one of them; he was the blacksmith's apprentice in Butterfield; a big, blond man, young and usually good-natured. His name was Al Hunt. But now he did not look good-natured.

Dan Corbett stopped near the war-wagon, gazed at the sweaty, haggard-looking men inside it, stiffly dismounted without a word, looped his reins at the rack and walked forward in the direction of the bunkhouse. He halted a couple of yards away and said, 'Come on out. It's Marshal Corbett. Singletary, you in there?'

The answer was gruff. 'Yeah. We're all in here but Ernie, and the sons of bitches killed him.'

'Leave the guns behind,' replied Corbett in an inflectionless, bitter voice, 'and come on out.'

Singletary might have consented, but someone in there was not ready to surrender. He said, 'Marshal; you disarmed those crazy bastards in that big old wagon?'

Corbett was not in a argumentative mood. '*Come out*! This damned fight is over.'

Dick Chase walked over to stand beside Sam Picket, who was methodically re-loading his handgun. There were shiny brass cartridge casings underfoot. Sam raised his eyes, looked past Corbett at the doorless bunkhouse and said, 'I wouldn't trust those men in there under any circumstances.' He then slid the re-loaded sixgun into its holster, and leaned to watch.

Frank and Gus were resting comfortably, with Winchesters snugged back against their shoulders, waiting. They were ignoring the marshal. Those two possemen who had ridden from town with Dan Corbett walked up to the tailgate, looked in and one of them, the powerfully muscled-up blacksmith's apprentice, said, 'You fellers un-cock them guns and lean 'em aside.'

Gus Hanson turned just his head. He and the younger man looked stonily at one another, then Gus eased down his hammer, stepped back and dropped his Winchester atop the trampled blankets of the war-wagon.

Jim Jones picked up a canteen and drank, then handed the canteen to Frank Longtree.

From within the bunkhouse Singletary called to Marshal Corbett. 'We're comin' out . . . They'll try to shoot us.'

Dan's retort was sharp. 'No one's goin' to shoot you. Hurry it up.'

The first man to walk out of the log building

was a lean, narrow-faced rangerider with a sweat-darkened shirt. His holster was empty and he kept both hands up front. His close-spaced eyes flicked from Corbett to the men in the wagon, and the pair of possemen who were standing slightly away, on the east side of the wagon.

Corbett pointed. 'Stand still. Put your hands down.'

The other men came out. Singletary was last, and before he had stopped moving he launched into a blisteringly profane denunciation of Dick Chase, his rangemen, and the wagon they had used to dupe Singletary and his men.

Corbett abruptly said, 'That's enough, John. *Shut up!*' Corbett had the initiative, was in charge and would not have relinquished his position of authority regardless of what anyone said.

He told the rustlers to go over and stand in front of the barn, and while they were doing that Corbett stepped past the broken bunkhouse door, looked at the devastation inside, wrinkled his nose because of the powerfully pungent stench of black-powder gunsmoke, then turned back.

Dick Chase rolled and lit a smoke, then accepted a canteen from Gus Hanson, drank deeply, and jerked his head as Dan Corbett approached. 'There's another one in the barn. He's got a hell of a leg-wound.'

122

Corbett strode in there. While he was examining the wounded man, the other men stood awkwardly in bleak silence, looking at one another. The pair of possemen were the only men with weapons in their hands, and they let them hang at their sides, but watched the other men closely, as though they would not have hesitated to shoot if trouble started again.

Dan Corbett walked back out into the late-day reddish light, stopped and looked around. His body slackened a little. He shoved back his hat, then he turned slowly toward John Singletary. After looking at the unarmed man standing in front of the barn for a long time, he said, 'Tell me again about Barney goin' over to Denver to have his eyes examined.'

Singletary must have detected the hollowness in the lawman's voice because he said nothing for a while, then shrugged his shoulders before answering. 'What do you want me to tell you? I told you where he went yesterday. What more is there to tell?'

'He didn't leave out of Butterfield, John.'

'Well . . . all I know is that he said that was where he was goin' and—'

Corbett interrupted sharply. 'He didn't go to Denver.'

'He told me—'

'He's lyin' in Chase's barn under a dirty piece of old canvas, John, deader'n hell from a close-up shot in the back.'

123

For five seconds no one moved or spoke. Then Singletary made a bland statement. He said, 'I'm missin' a rider; name's Wes King. Find him; ask him about Barney. They had words.'

From inside the war-wagon the bound rustler's eyes widened in stunned disbelief. Jim Jones, standing close by, looked down. When their eyes met King said, 'That's a damned lie! Gawddammit, marshal, cut me loose and help me down out of here!'

Dick Chase did not wait for Marshal Corbett's reaction, he climbed into the wagon, wordlessly untied Wesley King, then helped him to his feet, and when he was visible to the men over in front of the barn, John Singletary calmly said, 'That's him, Dan. I sent him out lookin' for Mister Brackett last night and he never came back—an' you found Mister Brackett shot in the back. I told you, they had words.'

Wesley King got awkwardly down over the tailgate, his legs and arms had had minimum circulation for a long time. He had to support himself on the side of the wagon, but his blazing eyes and twisted features indicated that there was nothing wrong with his head. He stared steadily at Singletary when he denounced the man to Marshal Corbett.

'He told me he'd shot a rustler up in the foothills. He sent me up there last night, after the rest of us got back from the mountains. He told me to make a cairn of rocks over the carcass.'

Corbett was watching the indignant rangeman. 'Who was up there?' he asked.

'No one! Well, there wasn't no one in the ravine, but there had been.' King gestured. 'These fellers was waitin' and they caught me. There wasn't nobody in those rocks because these fellers and Mister Chase already had it over at their home-place in the barn.'

Corbett turned toward Dick, eyebrows raised. Dick explained how Gus and Jim had found the body and had brought it home in the old wagon. Corbett looked at Hanson. Gus looked steadily back, nodding his head without saying a word.

Singletary spoke up into the silence. 'Chase's men found Barney's carcass. But that don't explain how he died nor what took Wes so long after he left here to go lookin' for Barney.'

Dick smoked and gazed at the rustler with a dawning idea; perhaps one of the main reasons John Singletary had survived so long as an outlaw, was because he was not only clever and shrewd, and dangerous, but also because he was one of the best liars in creation. He knew exactly how to cast a doubt, which is what he had just done. Dick did not doubt for one minute but that Singletary had killed Barney Brackett, but he had sound reason to believe this; Dan Corbett had nothing to go on but the word of men who had been involved right from the beginning in all this, and at least one of them was an accomplished liar.

Dick dropped his smoke, stepped on it and said, 'Marshal; ask Singletary if he and Brackett did not ride into the foothills together yesterday, when Brackett was supposedly on his way to Denver—and only one of them rode back down out of there.'

Before Dan could speak, John Singletary put a stare upon Chase and said, 'That's right. We went into the foothills together to hunt for cattle, and because it was gettin' along in the day, Barney said he'd just head on out instead of comin' back to the ranch with me. He said it was a hell of a long ride over to Denver.'

Corbett turned toward Dick again, looking sceptical.

Frank Longtree spat, then spoke in disgust. 'Marshal, go look in the barn. Brackett's saddle's hanging in there.' Frank levelled a sulphurous look at John Singletary. 'You lyin' bastard, now you're goin' to tell us Mister Brackett rode to Denver bareback.'

Dan Corbett walked into the barn again. While he was gone Gus Hanson regarded Singletary from a tired, lined face set in an expression of complete loathing. He said, 'You worthless scum, I'm goin' to break your neck if the law don't!'

The posseman who worked for the blacksmith in town snarled at Gus. 'You shut

126

up! Any more out of you an I'm goin' to climb in there and turn you inside out!'

Gus turned. So did Jim and Frank and Sam. The blacksmith's apprentice was perhaps fifteen years younger than Gus. In size and heft they were equal. The younger man's blue eyes blazed with animosity. Gus turned back and leaned upon the side-board without a word.

Marshal Corbett emerged from the barn lugging a saddle with Brackett's initials on the cantle. He dumped it in the dust and looked over at Singletary. 'When you're goin' to hide something,' he said, 'don't shove it under a mound of hay because that's where a man would look first.'

Now, Dick thought, Dan Corbett's mood had changed. But Singletary was not the least dismayed. He said, 'If you know Barney Brackett, Marshal, why then you know that's his *workin'* saddle, not his *ridin'* saddle. He was using his *good* saddle yesterday.'

Corbett came right back. 'Then why try to hide this one in the hay?'

Singletary shrugged. 'Ask Wes King, he was the one who planned to murder Mister Brackett.'

Wesley King stared in absolute disbelief at John Singletary. Before he could make a protest, one of the other captives casually said, 'That's right, Marshal. Wes an' me did a lot of ridin' together. He tol' me a couple of times

Mister Brackett had braced him real hard, and by gawd he didn't take that from no one; that he'd settle up with Mister Brackett for that.'

King was staring at the man who had said that. The captive looked back, almost casually and certainly dispassionately. He was the same narrow-faced man with the bright, closely-spaced eyes who had been the first man to walk out of the bunkhouse. Now, he brought forth the makings and went to work rolling a smoke.

Dick Chase heard Sam mutter something. He ignored that to shift his attention back to Singletary. He had heard a number of times how men that clever had eluded not just a hang-rope, but prison as well. He said, 'What about the cattle, Singletary? What about gettin' rid of Mister Brackett's riders, then hiring your partners so's you could rustle Brackett's cattle? And what about Scaggs, the feller you sold those cattle to and forged bills of sale for?'

Dan Corbett leaned to listen as the heretofore silent posseman spoke, then the marshal cocked an eye at the sky and said, 'Al, you an' Tom round up some horses for these fellers. We're goin' back to town.' Then as his posseman headed toward the barn and the corrals out back, Corbett also said, 'John, you and your riders are under arrest . . . Mister Chase; you too. Shuck your gun. You an' your riders—shuck your guns and climb down out

128

of that wagon.'

Dick and his men stared. Jim Jones made a high-pitched protest and Marshal Corbett got red in the face as he fiercely gestured with an upraised fist. 'Get down out of that wagon! Leave your weapons in there! *Get down*!'

Sam Picket, who had known Marshal Corbett for a long time, quietly said, 'What for, Dan? What you chargin' us with?'

Corbett turned sharply. 'How about attackin' Brackett's place, Sam? How about killin' one of his riders?'

That surprised everyone. Instead of protesting that they had attacked *Singletary*'s gang of rustlers, when they stared at Corbett he said, 'That feller in the barn is dead.'

Dick Chase felt this announcement as though it were a physical blow. He had not actually thought the wounded man would die. That he *had* died meant that he had been weaker than he had seemed to be, and yet in spite of this, and perhaps the fact that the rustler had suspected he was going to die, the black-eyed man had cursed Dick Chase right up to his last few moments. That kind of toughness was rare. Dick looked down the dark runway, barely made out the lumpy shape near the rear barn opening, and wagged his head. It was hard not to respect that kind of toughness.

It required time to catch and saddle horses for the men in front of the barn. Dusk was close, in fact, before Dan Corbett gave the order to mount up. He had Jim Jones climb to the high seat of the war-wagon and lead off out of the yard in the direction of Butterfield, but they had not traversed more than a mile before the wagon's slowness had annoyed Marshal Corbett sufficiently to make him lead the cavalcade of horsemen on ahead. He detached his quiet posseman to remain back with Jim Jones.

It was very late before the riders reached town, but there were still a few people abroad, mostly over at the saloon where all-night poker sessions were not unusual, so the large party of horsemen walking their mounts through starlight down in front of the jailhouse was not unobserved. By mid-morning tomorrow Butterfield would be alive with rumours, wild guesses, and gossip.

CHAPTER THIRTEEN

QUESTIONS AND ANSWERS

The only professional man in Butterfield was the medical practitioner; there was no lawyer and there had never been one. A circuit-riding judge appeared routinely in Butterfield once a month, and if Marshal Corbett had a prisoner and a complaint His Honour would hold court either at the poolhall, which would be cleared out for the occasion, or over at the fire-hall, which was larger and was commonly used for civic affairs.

But first Dan had to write out the complaint, and since he abhorred this aspect of his duties he usually laboured long over it, and emerged at the conclusion in a foul mood.

He was not in a good mood anyway, after taking breakfast over to the jailhouse for his prisoners, following his own first meal of the day, because not just the caféman, but several of the other early diners, had queried him at great length concerning a story going around the community about him having returned to town late last night with a whole passel of unarmed men followed by a big old oaken wagon, as ugly as original sin, which was hauling a lot of guns in it, and a dead man.

When he got settled in his dingy little front office with a cup of black coffee from the pot atop his office wood-stove, he sat a long time in thought, then went down to the cells and brought Dick Chase back to the office with him. He scowled as though expecting Chase to heap indignation on him. Instead, Dick sat on a wall-bench, rubbed his stubbly jaw and said, 'That's the first night's sleep I've had in a long time.' Then Dick smiled a little. 'Even the gunny-sacks full of straw you got for mattresses over those rope springs felt good.'

Dan sat down, looked at his cup, then stood

131

up again. 'You care for a cup of Java?'

Dick declined and went to work rolling a smoke. He was not the least impatient nor irritable; at least he did not appear to be.

Dan re-seated himself and clasped big hands atop the desk as he gazed at the rancher. 'There was a lot of talk out there last night.'

Dick nodded, trickled smoke and waited.

'I had to lock the whole passel of you up. You understand that, don't you?'

Again Dick calmly nodded his head without speaking.

Marshal Corbett shifted slightly in his chair. 'Tell me, right from the beginning, what you did and why you did it. Don't leave anythin' out.'

Dick talked for fifteen minutes in an unhurried, measured manner. When he had completed his recitation he had done exactly as Corbett had asked him to do; he had not omitted anything. Then he put out his smoke and said, 'Wes King didn't shoot Brackett. You should have seen his face when he came back into the cook-shack.'

Corbett sighed. 'Maybe not, but the look on a man's face isn't evidence of a hell of a lot. And the circuit-rider who holds court in Butterfield has icewater for blood. If King didn't do it, the proof's got to be better'n just the look on his face.'

Dick said, 'All right, Marshal. I'll give you

some proof ... You shoot a man in the back on a clear, quiet day in open country using a sixgun—one of the noisiest guns around—and anyone will hear the noise for a couple of miles.'

'Meaning?'

'Meaning King couldn't have done it last night because my crew and I were up near those foothills looking for Brackett's grave. We'd have heard any loud noise, but especially a gunshot. There are Sam Picket, Frank Longtree, Gus Hanson and I who will swear under oath there was no gunshot up there.'

Corbett gazed a long while at his clasped hands, then raised his head again. 'About the cattle, Mister Chase ...'

'When you talk to Singletary's men, ask them about a feller named Scaggs who's been buying Brackett beef for months. Especially talk to Wes King. He's so mad at the others he'll do what he can to help you find Scaggs.'

'I got to prove John Singletary did this, Mister Chase.'

'Find Scaggs, get copies of those bills of sale Singletary gave him, and compare the handwriting to Brackett's handwriting—*if* Singletary forged Brackett's name.' Dick crookedly smiled. 'But I'll lay you a good bet that he didn't forge Brackett's signature. The more I listened to Singletary yesterday over in the ranch-yard, the more I believe he's too smart to forge a bill of sale. He would sign them himself as Brackett's foreman, with authority to peddle cattle and sign bills of sale.' Dick's smile lingered, humourless and wry. 'Brackett's dead, Marshal.'

'I know that.'

'Have you guessed why?'

Corbett reddened slightly and pursed his lips. He did not like the way this was going. Chase was making good sense; he was politely telling Dan Corbett he was better at this sort of guesswork than Dan was.

'I'll tell you why I think Singletary shot Brackett in the back and killed him. Because either Brackett was beginning to realise that his cattle were disappearing, or else perhaps because he knew Singletary was signing those bills of sale.'

Dan Corbett sighed and threw himself back in his old swivel chair. He gazed at Dick Chase for a long time before speaking. 'He wouldn't have had to kill Barney. Him and his crew could just saddle up and ride out.'

'No, Marshal; they hadn't finished yet. They still had my long yearlings to steal, and maybe other cattle in the basin. But—and this is what I think. With Brackett dead, Singletary can stand up in court and say he had Brackett's permission to sell cattle and sign bills of sale. Brackett's not around to say that's a damned lie.' Dick leaned to arise from the bench. 'Marshal, I don't think you're goin' to get a conviction against Singletary for being a rustler. Not if he can hire even a two-bit attorney. Like you said, you got to have proof, and the best you're goin' to be able to come up with—if you're lucky—is some shady cattle buyer named Scaggs who'll lie himself into hell to keep from being implicated.'

Dick stood up, still wearing that crooked little smile.

Corbett leaned back across the room regarding the younger man from an expressionless face. Eventually he said, 'I sure hope you're wrong.' Then he shot up to his feet, picked up the cell keys and marched Dick back down where he locked him in, unlocked John Singletary's cell and jerked his head for the outlaw to precede him up into the little office.

He did the same with Singletary as he had done with Dick Chase, to put him at ease he offered hot coffee. Singletary, unlike Chase, accepted, took the cup to a chair, sat down and smiled at Corbett. It was a confident smile with some maliciousness showing in it. He tasted the coffee and said, 'Good brew, Dan.'

Corbett ignored that, sat staring at the hard-faced, dark-eyed man in the chair for a while, then said, 'Tell me everything that happened yesterday when Chase and his crew came over to the ranch, John. And don't leavin anythin' out.'

Singletary had had all last night and part of this morning to perfect what he had to say. He talked glibly, using even more time than Dick Chase had used, and when he eventually finished, strode to the stove to re-fill his coffee cup.

Dan Corbett, who seldom smoked, fished around in a desk drawer for a sack of dust-dry tobacco, troughed a paper and went thoughtfully to work. By the time he had lit up, Singletary was back in his chair with his fresh coffee. He looked perfectly confident. He even smiled when Dan coughed after his first inhalation.

'Chewing is better for a man,' he said.

Corbett was a stubborn man, he continued to smoke the strong tobacco. 'Tell me about sellin' Brackett's cattle, John,' he said, and leaned as he had done before, big hands clasped together atop the desk.

'Mister Brackett's eyes been goin' bad for a long time, Dan. Maybe you knew that. It wasn't a secret. I been after him for dang near a year to go over to Denver and have them looked at.'

'What's that got to do with you sellin' his cattle, John?'

'I'm coming to that,' replied Singletary, and sipped his coffee before speaking again. 'He figured he was goin' blind. I think he was, but I never told him that. Anyway, we had a long talk and he decided to sell off his cattle first, then later, he figured to sell the ranch too, and move into town where he'd be near a doctor

136

and all . . . He told me to look into sellin' off the cattle. He give me authorisation to sell 'em for him.'

'To sign bills of sale, Dan?'

'Yeah. He told me to sign the bills of sale for him too.' Singletary finished his second cup of coffee and put the cup upon the corner of Corbett's desk.

Dan sat looking at his clasped hands for a while before asking another question. 'When you'n Barney was riding in the foothills yesterday . . .'

'Lookin' for cattle. He wanted to ride out; it was a fine day an' he hadn't been out of the yard in weeks. So I told him I thought there was some strays somewhere up there and he wanted to go with me to hunt them.'

'On his good saddle?'

'Yes. Like I just told you, Dan, he was feelin' pretty good yesterday, so he was riding his best horse and his best saddle.'

'An' he left you up in there headin' for Denver?'

'Yeah. He told me there wasn't no point in goin' back to the ranch; he'd just head out from up there and save himself maybe ten, fifteen miles of riding.'

Corbett's eyes were fixed upon Singletary when he said, 'Without no razor, nor bedroll, nor change of pants, Dan?'

For just a second Singletary faltered, then he said, 'Dan, you knew Barney as well as I

137

did. Maybe better, in fact. He did things pretty much on the spur of the moment.'

Silence settled with Corbett gazing steadily at John Singletary. 'For a fact,' he eventually said quietly, 'I knew Barney very well . . . All right, now tell me why you sent Wesley King up into the foothills last night.'

'After Mister Brackett and I parted and I was ridin' along, I came onto this feller scoutin' up the range. I watched him from behind a hill for a while. He was lookin' for cattle. When I was sure of that I jumped out my horse and took after him. He run northward up the ravine like he was tryin' to reach the mountains. He took two shots at me.'

Corbett slowly eased back off the desk. 'He shot at you?'

'Twice. I stopped, got down with my Winchester, and nailed him dead centre. Then I dumped him down into the ravine and piled a few rocks on him, but it was gettin' along toward evening so I headed for home and sent Wes King back up there to finish the job. Nothing wrong with shootin' a rustler who was shootin' at me, Dan.'

Corbett said, 'No, I'd say there wasn't, John.' He dragged those words out. Then he spoke again the same drawn-out drawl. 'Barney was riding his best horse and his good saddle?'

'Yes.'

'John . . . I know that horse. He's won more stake-races in Tenino basin than any other animal.'

Singletary nodded agreement. It did not occur to him, until Marshal Corbett made his next statement, that he had been baited.

'John; you didn't send Wesley King up there into the foothills until after dark . . . By that time if Barney had been heading overland toward Denver he would have been a hell of a long way up through the mountains. Ten, maybe fifteen miles. And it was dark last night, even here in town where we got lights. There wasn't a moon, John . . . But King found Barney, shot him in the back, then rode back down by that place where you'd buried the rustler, and got caught by Chase's crew.'

Singletary gave a delayed, measured answer. 'All I know is that I sent Wes up there, and that he an' Mister Brackett had had words. I'm sure he found Mister Brackett and shot him in the back. I'm as sure of that as I am that I'm sittin' here right now.'

Corbett's face showed expression for the first time. He showed square, big white teeth and a wolfish grin. 'I'm not, John, because Chase's crew found Barney right where you said you dumped that rustler, and if King had bushwhacked Barney in the mountains he wouldn't have lugged the carcass back down to that ravine. No bushwhacker in his right mind would do a thing like that. I've known a lot of them, John, and I've never known one that crazy . . . But even if King *did* do that—'

'What the hell are you hintin' at, Dan?' demanded Singletary, showing a hard brightness in his dark eyes.

'Let me finish,' stated Corbett. 'Even if King had done that—I examined Barney in Chase's barn last night. He'd been dead a lot longer than since last night, so, whoever killed him didn't do it after nightfall.'

Singletary hung fire for the second time, then gave his shoulders a careless shrug. 'All right. Maybe Wes found Mister Brackett earlier, and shot him then.'

Dan Corbett arose with the keys in his hands, and with a glint in his eyes. 'After I lock you up, I'll talk to the other fellers who ride for you. They can tell me if Wesley King left there on the ride back down from the mountains. Get up, John.'

Singletary arose slowly, his eyes slipping past Corbett to the rack of rifles, carbines and shotguns over against the opposite wall. Corbett was between him and the gun-rack, and Corbett was armed. Singletary turned and walked ahead of the marshal back down into the cell-room.

When Corbett herded Wesley King up to his office the younger man was in a venomous mood. He did not sit down, and as soon as they were alone, the cell-room door closed behind them, he launched into a long

140

recitation of accusations against Singletary and the other rustlers. He went back three years to his first meeting with Singletary, and what he and the others had done with Singletary since then, and finally, when Dan Corbett got the opportunity, he drew off a cup of coffee, passed it to the agitated younger man and pointed to the same bench Dick Chase had used.

'Sit down,' he said. 'Now then, I know you fellers are cattle thieves. I'm goin' to haul you up before a judge for that, but Barney Brackett was a friend of mine, an' I want the man who bushwhacked him.'

King did not taste the coffee, but he sat over there holding the cup. 'Singletary shot him.'

'Can you prove it?'

'He's dead, ain't he, and they was riding alone together in the foothills, wasn't they? An' only Singletary come back, didn't he?'

Corbett did not answer. Instead he asked another question. 'When you were up there along that ravine where the grave was, did you fire a gun?'

King slowly lowered the cup and stared. 'Fire a gun? You mean at Chase and—?'

'I mean just what I said: Did you fire a gun? For whatever reason, did you fire your gun?'

'No. Hell. Mister Chase come out from behind a bent pine tree before I knew he was within thirty miles of me. Then his riders come up too. I couldn't even have drawed my gun let alone got off a shot.'

'Where is your gun?'

'I don't know. Mister Chase taken it off me and pitched it down the ravine.'

'It's still up there?'

'As far as I know it is. No one went down lookin' for it last night. After they caught me, we all headed for the Dutra place.'

Dan looked at the coffee cup. 'Drink it down,' he said, and stood up. But Wes King did not even look at the cup, he was watching Marshal Corbett.

'Marshal,' he said in the calmest tone of voice he had used thus far in the jailhouse office, 'I never killed Mister Brackett. I never killed a man in my life. I've rustled a few head, but I never bushwhacked anyone in my damned life.'

Corbett gestured. 'If you're goin' to drink it, get it down, otherwise let's go back to the cells.'

'Marshal that's the gospel truth, I never in my life—'

'Gawddammit, get up—and shut up!'

When Corbett herded King back to a cell and locked him in, he stood a moment in the dingy little corridor looking past steel straps at John Singletary, then he turned, unlocked Dick Chase's cell and jerked his head. As Chase was heading back up the corridor Sam Picket said, 'Dan; how long is this goin' to last?'

Probably because they were friends Dan Corbett answered, otherwise he probably would not have. 'Not a hell of a lot longer, Sam. At least I hope not a hell of a lot longer.'

Up in the office Corbett flung his cell-room keys atop the desk and picked up his hat. 'We're goin' for a ride,' he told Dick. 'You're goin' to show me where that grave is—and where you threw that gun you taken off Wes King.'

They left the jailhouse together. Corbett turned back to lock the roadside door, and on the way to the liverybarn where the horses had been stabled last night, he stopped at the blacksmith's shop to tell Al Hunt, that muscular blond apprentice, where he was going, when he hoped to be back, and handed Hunt the doorkey as he also said, 'Feed 'em tonight, Al, and don't let any of 'em out, even to pee, and don't let anyone in to see 'em.'

Down at the liverybarn the marshal loosened a little, glanced at the position of the sun and said, 'Hell; I'm goin' to miss supper again tonight.'

The liveryman and his hostler rigged out their horses and watched with strong curiosity as Corbett and Dick Chase walked their animals northward up out of town. The hostler, who was an inveterate gossip, said, 'Mister Corbett's up to something sure as hell,' and the paunchy liveryman put a jaundiced look upon his employee and answered sarcastically. 'Is that a fact? I thought him and that Chase-feller was goin' to ride out so's they could admire the wild flowers.'

The heat was there, along with hot sunlight, the sky was as clear as crystal glass, without a blemish in it from horizon to horizon, and maybe that would not have pleased a lot of Tenino basin stockmen, who were never happy unless it was either raining in the summer or looked as though it would start raining soon; as far as Dan Corbett was concerned, the weather was ideal for a long ride.

He told Dick about the weapon he wanted to examine, and Chase smiled. He was sure he could find it in the underbrush down the side of the ravine. But he was also smiling because it pleased him to realise that big Dan Corbett, for whom he had not felt a great deal of respect nor admiration, was turning out to be a much more astute and shrewd man than Dick had thought he was.

'It's up there,' he said, and also said, 'If that's the kind of proof you need, how about Scaggs?'

Corbett rubbed his jaw before replying. 'I don't think I'll have to hunt him down.' He stopped rubbing and gazed at his companion. 'Y'know, Mister Chase, I wasn't real pleased when you came out here to run your uncle's place . . . I guess the best way for folks to get acquainted after they've made a wrong first judgment is to get into a mess like this and get

144

to figure one another out . . . By the way; where the hell did you find that big old oak wagon?'

Dick had expected Corbett to say something different, and now as he rode along studying the larger and older man, it occurred to him that he had indeed made a bad misjudgment about Marshal Corbett. It also occurred to him that Dan had just changed the subject because whatever else he had in mind about the Brackett killing, he was not ready to divulge it.

'It was in the wagon-shed at the ranch when I took over,' he replied. 'I think maybe my uncle used it in the early days out here, when there were Indians and renegades and no law.'

Corbett rode along thinking about that, and smiling. 'You want to sell it?' he asked.

Dick looked around in surprise. 'No. What would you use it for?'

'Maybe someday, for the same thing you used it for. A man never can tell, can he?'

Dick smiled. 'I'll loan it to you any time you want it.'

They angled a little so as to arrive in the foothills about where that gulch was, with Dick doing the guiding, and after a long silence Dan Corbett said, 'Singletary . . . I've known him since he arrived in the basin . . . You never know about people. Old Barney thought the world of him. Well; at least he did the last time I saw him, which would be about three, four months ago . . . Maybe on our way back we could sashay by your place and load Barney on a pack horse and fetch him back to town with us.'

Dick nodded without speaking. He was concentrating his attention upon the foothills. He had not been up there before he and his rangemen had gone up there looking for a grave, and the light had not been very good then. But like all rangemen, Dick Chase had a very good sense of direction.

CHAPTER FOURTEEN

DEATH!

Finding the ravine was not difficult, and riding up it in good daylight was easy; but when they tied their horses where scuffed earth and horse-droppings showed where Chase's crew had caught Wesley King, then went down the slope into the underbrush looking for the gun, they had trouble. For one thing Dick was only generally aware of the area where he had thrown the gun. He had been interested in the gun's owner, not the weapon itself, when he had flung it down there. For another thing, the underbrush was thick, wiry, had thorns, and as Dick Chase recalled, the gun had had all the bluing worn off it; it was uniformly grey.

Marshal Corbett stopped scuffing through

brush to wipe off sweat, squinted up where Dick was probing and said, 'You sure you didn't fling it farther down?'

Dick shook his head. 'No. Just keep looking.'

Dan Corbett kicked a booted foot under a particular clump of dense underbrush and found something. It was not the sixgun, it was a surprised and fierce old rattlesnake. He went into his coil in seconds, raised his head from the outer coil, raised his rattles from inside of his circle, and startled Marshal Corbett so badly that the lawman nearly fell into another patch of brush yielding ground.

Then he swore.

Dick paused to watch for a moment, then off-handedly said, 'I don't think it will be that far down the slope. Look uphill a little more.'

Corbett glared, mopped off sweat, teetered between killing the snake and walking away from it, and finally hiked back up the slope until he was parallel with Chase. They had about a half acre of ground to cover. They worked back and forth toward each other, and Dan snorted, stopped moving, then leaned with a cry of triumph. When he straightened up he was holding a battered old grey Colt in his hand.

Dick worked toward him as the marshal methodically opened the gate and slowly turned the cylinder. There was a cartridge in every chamber. He waited until Dick was beside him, then slowly turned the cylinder again so that his companion could also see that the gun was fully loaded. Then Dan sniffed the barrel, looked at Dick and said, 'All right. This here'll keep King's neck out of a noose,' and shoved the old gun into his waistband.

Dick cocked his head a little. 'That's proof that King *didn't* kill Brackett. If you're goin' to be hard-headed, Marshal, then you got to find something that'll prove Singletary *did* kill him.'

Corbett started up the slope to the top-out, and when he was catching his breath after the climb he said, 'Let's go get Barney and head for town.' He did not mention Singletary again until they were coming down into the Dutra yard, heading for the barn, and his companion offered to bring in a pack horse, then, as they were dismounting out front, Corbett said, 'I'll get it—if it exists.'

Dick looked across his saddle-seat. 'Get what?'

'Proof that John shot Barney in the back . . . You get us a horse and I'll tie Barney in that canvas you boys tossed over him.'

Nothing more was said until Dick brought in a big combination horse and began rigging it out to be packed and led. Then he said, 'Like I told you in the office, Marshal, Singletary is a smart man.'

Big Dan Corbett picked up the dead man, eased him across the horse's back, and went to work with a rope as he replied to that. 'I don't think you know how smart he is, Dick. When I had Wes King in the office, he told me about rustling and horse-stealin' John and his gang brought off over the past three years that would make your hair stand on end . . . And I sort of agree with you; I'd have a hell of a time nailing John for rustling—but I'm not goin' to even try to do that . . . Ten years ago they'd have hung him for that, but nowadays even a cranky judge like the one that'll hold the hearing in Butterfield, don't hang rustlers any more . . . I want John Singletary for murdering Barney Brackett. For *that*, by gawd, His Honour'll hang him so high birds won't be able to build nests in his hair. And I can get him for that.'

'How? What proof you got, Marshal?'

'I got his gun in a desk drawer.'

'He'll have re-loaded it, Marshal.'

'All right. I got Wes King to testify, along with your crew, who didn't hear a shot when you was close enough to have heard one, and I've got John's own statement that he and Barney rode up there together—just the two of them—and only one of 'em came back. And—'

'Marshal,' stated Dick, securing the last of the rope. 'All I know about the law you could put atop a nail-head without any crowding, but I know this much: So far all you've been talkin' about is circumstantial evidence. It sure as hell's not proof.'

Dan Corbett led the pack-horse out of the barn into slanting sunshine, and smiled as he swung across his own animal with the lead-shank in one big fist. 'I got something else,' he said, and turned his horse to commence riding out of the yard on the way back down to Butterfield. He did not say what the other thing was that he had, and since he did not volunteer the information, Dick did not pry for it.

It was late in the day but it was still warm. In fact it was downright hot, and as Dick slouched along he cast a sidelong glance at the brassy sky. There was not a breath of air stirring, there was a faint, diaphanous sheen to the heavens, the sun shone through it faintly red, and Dick went to work making a smoke as he casually said, 'It's goin' to rain, Marshal.'

Corbett looked up, nodded, and glanced around at the limp carcass wrapped like a cocoon in that soiled old piece of canvas. 'I'd like to know what Singletary did with all the money he got for Barney's cattle,' he said, and wagged his head. 'It must add up to a damned fortune.'

Dick was not very interested in that. 'Cached it more than likely. If he stayed out at the Brackett place supervising his gang, he didn't get much chance to spend it.'

Corbett smiled. 'That's about how I got it figured. And if I know John Singletary, and I think I do, he cached it on the ranch.'

Dick blew ash off the tip of his cigarette. 'He'll come back for it, Marshal.'

'The hell he will . . . That's goin' to be my proof. If Barney had given him authorisation to peddle those cattle, then John would have brought the money back to Barney. I don't believe he did that—he couldn't have, could he, because he was stealin' those cattle and sellin' them and Barney didn't know a darned thing about that—so—when I find the cache and take a sack full of money to court as proof that Singletary was rustlin' old Barney to death—'

'Marshal,' stated Dick Chase drily, as he leaned to punch out his smoke atop the saddlehorn. 'You're talkin' about proof that Singletary was a cattle-thief. Sure; if you can find the damned cache that might get him convicted as a rustler—but what you wanted was to get him hanged as a murdering bushwhacker.'

Dan Corbett lifted his head to scan the dying day for Butterfield's rooftops on ahead. 'That's how I'll do it,' he told Chase. 'How much money do you expect might be in his cache?'

'You're a cowman; you could make a better guess than I could.'

Dick thought a long time before answering. First, in order to give a decent estimate he would have to know about how many head of cattle Singletary had stolen and sold, and he had no idea about that, but he did know roughly what beef was bringing on the hoof this year, so he answered Corbett's question with a question of his own.

'How many head did Brackett run?'

Corbett frowned. 'I'll guess . . . A thousand head in all categories.'

Dick spat, straightened up in the saddle and finally said, 'I'll guess too . . . Seventy-five thousand dollars.'

Dan Corbett turned slowly and regarded his companion for a long time in total silence, then he sighed and faced forward again, watching the rooftops come a little closer. 'That's more money than I'd know how to count,' he said, almost reverently, then he became brisk, 'That's my bargaining equipment, Dick.'

Chase gazed at the older man. 'How?'

Corbett said, 'We were friends a long time. We can sit down and talk.'

'You mean whittle a stick?'

'Yeah.'

'Let him bribe you?'

'Yeah.'

'That's still not proof of murder.'

Corbett smiled, and angled so they would enter town by the alley behind his office, generally unseen from the main part of town. 'That's where you'll come in,' he said. 'He's goin' to admit to killin' Barney as part of the bribe—and you're goin' to be in the back room

152

off my office listening. Then you're goin' to tell His Honour what you heard.' Corbett was pleased with his scheme. As they picked their way past residences to the back-alley, he was smiling.

Dick Chase was not smiling. For one thing he was as hungry as a bitch wolf, for another thing he did not believe Singletary was going to be that easy to trap; and finally, he did not like the idea because it was entrapment pure and simple, and while the law turned a blind eye to devices of that nature, it left Dick Chase feeling uncomfortable. He wanted to see Singletary out-smarted, not out-manoeuvred.

Maybe he would feel better after he had eaten.

They carried Brackett's body into the backroom of the jailhouse and left it there, then they took the horses down to the liverybarn and left them, and finally they headed for the café, with its steamy front window.

They missed Butterfield's customary suppertime by about an hour, which neither of them objected to; and when the caféman saw Dick Chase with Marshal Corbett, although he was full of questions for Dan, he refrained from asking any of them, and instead concentrated on feeding them. The only remark he made was to the effect that he thought it was going to rain. They both agreed with him about that, and did not raise their heads again until they were finished eating, and Dan asked if Al Hunt had gotten food to take over to the jailhouse. The caféman said that he had, and Corbett paid for both the meals, nodded and walked out into the settling night, feeling expansive as he stood gazing in the direction of the jailhouse, where a light was burning.

Dick said, 'When do you figure to talk to Singletary?'

Corbett's answer was brusque. 'Now,' he said, and struck off toward the jailhouse.

They paused out front, exchanging a look. Evidently Dan Corbett had something in mind, but he did not express it—he did not have an opportunity. From inside, a hard, rough voice said, 'I got a right to see him,' and another, stronger, younger-sounding voice replied with equal intransigence. 'Whether you got a right or not, I'm not goin' to let you do it. When Marshal Corbett gets back—it'll be up to him.'

Dan faced the door wearing a puzzled scowl as he reached for the latch, shoved on inside with Dick Chase trailing him; that powerfully-built blacksmith's apprentice was standing behind the desk, staring woodenly at an older man, grey-headed and sharp-featured, who was attired in a dusty black suit-coat and matching britches. Neither of them was armed, as nearly as Dick could tell, and neither of them smiled when Dan walked in.

The blacksmith said, 'Marshal, this here is

Mister Scaggs. He come in a few minutes ago off the stage and says he's got a right to talk to John Singletary.'

Corbett eyed Scaggs, then faced the blacksmith with a nod of his head. 'I'm obliged to you for minding things, Al.'

After the powerfully put-together younger man departed, Corbett introduced Dick Chase to Scaggs, then he said, 'How did you know Singletary was in my jailhouse?'

Scaggs was already annoyed, so he simply transferred his irritation from the blacksmith's apprentice to Marshal Corbett. He looked out of pale, malevolent eyes when he replied. 'I was in town; heard somethin' about someone recognisin' Singletary among some fellers you brought to the jailhouse last night, and come down here a few minutes ago to see if it really was him.'

Corbett tossed his hat aside, went behind the desk and put Wes King's sixgun atop a pile of papers, then looked up. 'Do you want to know what he's charged with, Mister Scaggs?'

'Yes.'

'Murder and cattle stealing.'

Scaggs's sharp-featured face sagged. Clearly, Al Hunt had not told him why Singletary was being held. He looked around at Dick, who was standing by the door, looking on, then he looked back at Corbett. 'Murder . . . ?'

'Yeah. He killed Barney Brackett.'

Scaggs went to an old chair and sagged into it staring at the lawman. 'Brackett? I been buyin' cattle off Brackett for nigh onto a year now.' His pale eyes steadily widened. '. . . Cattle stealin'—for Chris'sake?'

Dick almost felt sorry for the greying older man. Either Scaggs was a consummate actor, which Dick doubted very much, or he was almost stunned with astonishment, and as he sat there staring, it was almost a certainty that he had just now arrived at a frightening conclusion. He had been buying stolen cattle.

He said, 'Good gawd,' and eased back in the chair.

'What are you doing in Butterfield?' asked Corbett.

For a while the livestock merchant did not make a sound, then his pale eyes came up again. 'I was goin' to hire a buggy an' drive out to the Brackett place; my boys been waitin' in camp several days now to pick up a little bunch of long yearlin' heifers Singletary was supposed to trail over to them . . . I was wonderin' if maybe somethin' went wrong . . . I had his money and the book from the Denver bank where he had them cheques of mine deposited. I was supposed to hand him the book next time we did business.'

Corbett walked over to the seated man and held out his hand. 'The bank book,' he said.

Scaggs dug it from a pocket and handed it over, then he reached with his other hand

156

inside another pocket and brought forth a pony of rye whiskey, from which he drank, then re-pocketed the little bottle. He watched Corbett flip through the bank book, then turn and toss the little book to Dick Chase. Corbett returned to his desk, sat down and said, 'We were off by ten thousand dollars, Dick. He got sixty-five thousand, not seventy-five thousand.' Then Corbett looked at the livestock buyer. 'When was the last time you talked to Barney Brackett?'

Scaggs flung out his arms. 'I never met the man in my life, Sheriff. I met John Singletary last autumn and we made the deal. He was representing Mister Brackett. I . . . you mean he stole—you mean he didn't have no authorisation to sell me those cattle, Sheriff?'

'Marshal, not sheriff,' stated Dan Corbett and hedged on a direct answer. 'If Mister Brackett didn't sign bills of sale, Mister Scaggs, and he never told you face-to-face Singletary could peddle cattle for him, you're up to your butt in trouble.'

Scaggs fairly blasted out his reply to that. 'For Chris'sake, I been buyin' cattle like that for thirty years, Sher-Marshal, and so help me this is the first time in my whole blasted life I ever had trouble about it. Lots of cowmen empower their foremen to—'

'An' you didn't think it was strange that Singletary had you deposit the money in a Denver bank to his account, Mister Scaggs.

'No! I been doin' that too, for a lot of years, for stockmen who live far out. I'm happy to oblige 'em. In my business, Marshal, you got to do a lot of little things for folks in order to keep their business, and I always—'

'Where are the cattle, Mister Scaggs?'

'Well . . . mostly they're hangin' on meat-hooks back east somewhere. I shipped the fat ones direct to Kansas City to the butchers. A few—like these long yearlin' heifers he was supposed to drive over—I peddled to ranchers around the country . . . My gawd, I can't believe John Singletary . . . He always seemed like a right decent and upstandin' feller.'

Corbett turned toward Dick Chase. 'We got the cache,' he said quietly. Dick nodded. 'And we got Mister Scaggs as a witness to the rustling operation.' He turned back toward the cattle buyer. 'I'm goin' to bring them to trial for rustling. I'll need you for a witness against 'em, Mister Scaggs, but the judge likely won't reach town for another month or so.'

Scaggs pulled out a big blue bandana to mop his face then lustily blew his nose before shoving the bandana back into a coat pocket. 'A month,' he muttered. 'Marshal, I cover a lot of country buyin' an' selling. Maybe in a month I'll be all the way down to—'

'I can lock you up as an accessory, Mister Scaggs.'

' . . . Marshal, I'll give you my address. You drop me a line the minute you know the judg⌐

158

is comin' to Butterfield and I'll be here. You got my word on it.'

Dan Corbett sat a long time studying the cattle buyer.

Finally, he stood up and pointed to a stub of a pencil on his desk, 'Write down the address on that scrap of paper, Mister Scaggs . . . You wanted to see Singletary—all right, set right there and I'll fetch him. I'd kind of like to see you two face each other.'

As Marshal Corbett picked up his keyring and crossed to the cell-room door, Scaggs went over, leaned across the desk and busily wrote while Dick Chase watched.

Without a warning a thunderous gunshot sounded down in the cell-room. Scaggs dropped the pencil and jumped. Dick, unarmed, heard a volley of profanity and shouldered Scaggs aside to reach the wall-rack where he snatched a loaded Colt off a wooden peg and turned toward the cell-room door.

He was waiting, watching the open oaken door, reluctant to step over there where he would be outlined by the light from the office, when the loud scuffing of hurrying booted feet came out to him. He cocked the Colt, stepped closer to the wall, and when John Singletary sprang into the room and saw Scaggs, and the livestock-buyer made a squawking sound at sight of the cocked sixgun in Singletary's right fist, Dick yelled out.

'Drop it!'

159

Singletary whirled; whether he had expected to see another man in the office or not, his mistake was to look at Scaggs instead of elsewhere. Now, he tried to correct that error by swinging the cocked Colt.

Dick squeezed the trigger. The explosion was deafening in that small room. Singletary yanked his trigger as a reflex; he was already stumbling violently under a solid impact. The bullet went into the ceiling. Singletary fell over a bench, landed in a sprawl with the sixgun easing out of his relaxing hand. He had been hit squarely in the middle of the chest.

Now, there was not a sound down in the dingy little cell-room until a voice Dick recognised as belonging to Sam Picket called out 'Dick? Dick, you up there? Get some help if you are, he shot Marshal Corbett.'

Chase stepped over, looked at his victim, kicked the gun away, then turned on Scaggs. 'You know where the doctor lives?'

Scaggs did not know. 'I ain't very familiar with Butterfield.'

'Go ask around; find him and fetch him back here, *and run!*'

Scaggs flung open the door and disappeared in the darkness. Dick hesitated a moment, wondering whether he would ever see Mister Scaggs again, then he called down into the cell-room. 'Sam! Anyone else down there got a gun?'

Picket's answer was slightly delayed.

'They're shakin' their heads, Dick. All the same, bring a scattergun.'

It was good advice. Dick tossed the sixgun aside, took down a shotgun with a fourteen-inch barrel, and moved into the cell-room doorway. No one moved nor made a sound. Marshal Corbett was lying in a heap just outside an open cell door. Gus Hanson made a growly observation. 'He isn't dead, Dick, but he sure bounced off the cell behind him when that bullet hit him. I think he took it in the ribs . . . Get them damned keys and let us out of here.'

Dick went ahead, leaned over Dan Corbett, could see the lawman's chest rising and falling, then knelt. Gus growled for the keys again. Dick picked up the ring and handed it to Sam Picket, whose cell was closest, then he eased Corbett over until he could locate the source of bleeding. Gus had been right, the bullet had grooved a gory, bloody gash alongside the lawman's rib-cage. Dick raised his head as his riders freed themselves. 'Lend a hand,' he told them.

The cattle thieves were like statues as Chase and his riders carried the lawman to his office and put him on the floor up there in better light.

Dick tore the cloth away to fully expose the wound, then accepted some cloth from Jim Jones to staunch the flow of blood with. Frank Longtree quietly said, 'Gus—Sam—here he is.'

Frank was looking at John Singletary.

The doctor came hurrying in. He was a short, wiry grizzled man, and the way he gave orders and shoved men aside it was clear that this was a long way from being his first gunshot wound.

Dick stood up wiping his hands and looking down as the doctor went grimly and swiftly to work. Then Dick raised his eyes. 'Where did Singletary get that gun?' he asked.

No one knew, but Frank Longtree, who had been in the adjoining cell, said, 'When we heard you fellers talkin' up here in the office, Singletary went over with his back to us, back by the little barred, high window, and seemed to me to be tuckin' in his shirt-tails. Then, when Corbett came along, he stepped to the front of his cell—with a damned gun in his hand, and shot the marshal right in front of his cell . . . I don't believe those other rustlers had any idea he had a hide-out weapon, Dick. They was as stunned as I was. I could see their faces. They was standin' there like they'd turned into stone.'

The doctor arose. 'I'll need help getting him hauled to his quarters at the roominghouse.' He pointed a finger at Gus, Jim and Frank. 'Pick him up. Be careful; I've got most of the bleedin' stopped but if you joggle him very much it'll come through the bandages. Come along, I'll follow along.'

As Gus, Frank and Jim leaned to lift the

162

large lawman, even Gus had to grunt. As they were easing out the door with their inert burden, Dick saw the cattle-buyer in the shadows just beyond. He waited until they had Dan Corbett outside, then he stepped over to Scaggs and said, 'You won't have to worry about appearing against Singletary, but I reckon the marshal'll want you to testify against the rest of his gang.

Scaggs bobbed his head. He was still shaken; he had every right to be. '. . . The address is on the desk, like Mister Corbett wanted—if he lives . . .'

'He'll live,' stated Dick Chase, still sceptical of Scaggs. 'I sure hope you come up here when he writes you, Mister Scaggs . . . I'd hate to have to come lookin' for you.'

Scaggs's pale eyes considered the man he had just seen kill John Singletary. In an almost fervent voice he said, 'I'll come, Mister Chase. S'help me I'll be on the next stage after I hear from him. You got my word on that . . . Good night.'

Dick ignored Singletary's corpse, closed and barred the cell-room door, went to the desk to re-examine that Denver bankbook, then tossed it down and reached for his tobacco sack and papers. They'd found Singletary's cache—purely by accident, but still they had found it. And there would be no need for a murder trial now. He lit up, considered the ajar door, walked out in the direction of the roominghouse, and on the stroll up there decided that tomorrow or the next day he and his crew would go up and reclaim those mis-branded long yearlings, drive them home, re-work their marks, then get back to the business of cow ranching.

Across the roadway, out front of the saloon, about a dozen men were standing in shadows watching Dick Chase walk past upon the far plankwalk. By tomorrow the stories would begin, each more lurid than the last.